About the Author

Shelley G. Lockett has always dreamt of writing a book, and thanks impart, to an in-depth conversation with a work colleague, the structure and storyline of her saga evolved.

Now a widow, writing has become both her work and primary passion. Nevertheless, she tries to make time for faith, family, friends and finds her soul nourished when cooking on a volunteer basis. Whilst part two tidies up some loose ends. It also hints as to where the third volume in her trilogy might take those who are kind and free-minded enough to wish to read it.

The Last Known Plain
Part One: Founding Members

Shelley G. Lockett

The Last Known Plain
Part One: Founding Members

Olympia Publishers
London

www.olympiapublishers.com
OLYMPIA PAPERBACK EDITION

A CIP catalogue record for this title is
available from the British Library.

ISBN: 978-1-80074-310-6

This is a work of fiction.
Names, characters, places and incidents originate from the writer's
imagination. Any resemblance to actual persons, living or dead, is
purely coincidental.

First Published in 2023

Olympia Publishers
Tallis House
2 Tallis Street
London
EC4Y 0AB

Printed in Great Britain

Dedication

To my upright man.

PROLOGUE
THE STORY TELLER: 2010 THE YEAR OF THE GIGGLE

The stunning vista arrayed before them kept the two men who stood on the dusty ground of a small asteroid, which drifted between the third planet of the solar system and its equally dust covered moon, in satisfied silence until the younger of the pair tilted his head towards his father to ask, 'How about a story Dad?'

'Why certainly my boy,' the First to Be and Creator of All replied. 'Once in living history on a planet much like yonder one below...'

Dimples appeared on either side of his well-sculpted lips as the only Sinless One interrupted with a boyish laugh, 'I love that place. It's where I was born.'

'Thou knowest... I remember it well.'

Dismayed by the hollow sadness permeating throughout his father's barely audible words, Bro whispered, 'Alas it needed to be done,' and because he understood it was the memory of his overly cruel death, not the sweet joy of his conception that was the reason two diamond studded tears escaped from the outer corners of his parent's luminous eyes he quickly added a far lighter, 'I've been dead for thousands of years, Dad, so please beloved no more tears.'

Unable to dispute the truth of these words the ageless man

brushed the moisture from his face. Materialising a pair of finely crafted rocking chairs he waited until they were both comfortably seated before returning to the start of his tale.

'Once in living history on a planet much like yonder one below, a heart shaped island nestled beneath a large continent. Within this isle a small woman sat at a wooden desk, her capable hands poised above the keyboard of her computer. This is what she wrote and where she prayed her own story would one day end...'

PART ONE
FOUNDING MEMBERS

The conical vortex of energy which heralded the arrival of a tiny female held captive within the eye of its tumultuous mass, dissipated almost as suddenly as it had come. Fleeing while the woman's cowled gown of rich purple velvet settled in elegant folds around a pair of dainty slippers, and her quivering hand reached for the links of pewter that circled her thin white neck.

Michaela struggled with a sudden wall of dizziness as she raised the droplet of burnished metal suspended from the centre of the necklet to her colourless lips. Gently kissing the portrait of a whimsical cockatiel and the equally appealing hermit crab etched into its smooth surface. She hoped they would soon be free to aid her and the other chosen ones as they tackled one of the Afterlife's biggest challenges.

Throughout the centuries after her original death, she'd often journeyed back and forth amongst the different plains. Some had been for pleasure, but far more were at her Master's behest, thus she was well used to the pitfalls of travelling aloft. Yet regardless of the reason, never before had her arrival been accompanied by so much pageantry nor discomfort.

Thanks for that, Bro. Nothing like a bout of bloody nausea to make a person work harder, she silently muttered to herself, hastily covering her mouth when her roiling belly threatened to expel the last meal she'd eaten, and a series of violent shudders wracked her body. *Flopping oath what's with this plain, Master? Or is this your bloody idea of fun? Not even the worst of flaming drivers would normally make me feel this bloody bilious.*

Ending her vulgar tirade with a sullen grunt, Michaela pivoted far quicker than her upset tummy appreciated to rapidly survey the rectangular chamber she now stood in.

Devoid of both windows and doors, walls of pale lilac separated the room's high arched ceiling from its polished floorboards. In the centre of the longer eastern one stood an ornate inglenook. The gentle heat radiating out from the small fire burning between its soot-blackened bricks the room's only visible source of heating. On either side of the fireplace's carved mantelpiece a pair of pewter sconces encased squat candles. Their subtle light and the fire's dancing flames having little impact on the room's deeply shadowed corners.

Six chairs and a plain wooden table filled one end of the chamber. Its counterpart home to two women and three men, all lying on a half-circle of mauve leather couches.

Recognising each of the faces she could see, Michaela let out a sigh of relief as she walked over to sit beside her soulmate then lightly stroked his forehead while carefully chanting the words she'd been instructed to utter.

Although, the sound of his wife's soft voice seemed to beckon from a long way away and had to compete with his own rebellious stomach, William slowly opened his eyes.

'Hi sexy,' he murmured with a wan smile. 'Where are we?'

'Welcome to somewhere dear one... We've moved on again.'

'Bugger, I was really getting to like that place.'

'Mmm, I'd noticed,' Michaela grinned. The hand she'd used to pluck a piece of glittering tinsel from behind William's ear moved down to his broad chest as she added, 'No stay put dear one. If you feel as bad as you look, you'll want a few minutes to settle your tum… And there's four more I need to see too.'

But disregarding her words of caution William sat up. His face paling even further when another wave of nausea ran from the top of his silver flecked hair to the toes of the wine-coloured boots he wore.

'Four more? Sure you don't want some help?'

'Thanks, but no thanks. Apparently, this one's all mine and besides… I doubt the Boss is out of hearing range.'

'Ooow in that case, if you really don't need me…'

With a sympathetic shake of her head Michaela cautiously rose to her feet. Going from couch to couch, she touched each of the next three prone figures on their foreheads whilst repeating the same chant over and over.

Shite Master, she cursed in disgust when the unpleasant odour wafting up from the last to be woken made her stomach churn again. *Couldn't you have at least given him a shower before he left his previous plain?*

Making a mental note to put in for hazard credits Michaela bent over the large man, the only one of the five to be lying face down, and reluctantly brushed aside a shoulder length hank of greasy red curls.

Her finger barely touching the grimy skin of his neck as she hurriedly crooned, 'Remember what you can and be who you are.'

Thankfully, the sudden twitching of the man's extremities and the muffled utterings that came from his half-buried face

13

assured her he was at least stirring. So, with a grimace of distaste, she pulled a lace handkerchief from the side pocket of her gown and was still busily wiping the lavender scented cloth over both hands when she once again propped herself on the edge of William's couch.

'Bro forgot to give that one a bath,' she said in answer to his raised eyebrow.

'I wouldn't bet on that, babe. You know our illustrious Master's not above inserting his own, er, touch to an event.'

'True, but he damn well shouldn't... The man pongs worse than a bloody outhouse in summer.'

Not feeling up to debating the whimsy of their Master's humour nor wishing to see his soulmate's obvious ire directed towards himself, William stoically refrained from chastising her choice of language as he carefully sat up and placed an arm around her narrow shoulders.

'What now?' He murmured. 'Who's in charge, you?'

'For tonight anyway, the future is anyone's guess.'

In a flurry of action, the tiny woman rose to her feet and clapped her hands, then once most eyes had turned her way said, 'Good evening, everyone. In case you've forgotten... My name's Michaela and we've all passed on again. If the norm applies your memories may be a bit hazy at the moment and you're possibly feeling somewhat unwell... However, we've been given the rest of the night to get acquainted, or methinks in most cases reacquainted, as our environmental course doesn't commence until tomorrow morning. And after everyone's given us a short outline of who you are, we'll have a bite to eat.'

When all but the red-haired man nodded their agreement. Michaela resettled herself on the edge of her soulmate's couch.

Her fond smile and an out held palm a silent request for the young woman lying on the next divan to speak.

'Hi everyone, I'm Kat from the twentieth-century and all's good,' the petite blond shyly announced while waving her hand to and fro. This slight movement enough to make the orange sleeve of her blouse slip backwards to reveal a forearm decorated with several intricately coloured tattoos.

Foregoing any further personal details Kat quickly turned to address the woman sitting cross-legged on the divan to the left of her own. 'Sorry, I'm sure I've met you, unfortunately for the moment your name eludes me…'

Dressed in navy cargo pants and matching tee shirt, with fingernails painted the same bright crimson as the toes peeping from the front of her narrow-heeled sandals, the svelte lady was a picture of understated elegance.

'Yes, we have. I'm also from the twentieth-century and I've had heaps worse pass overs,' she softly exclaimed. Her large, emerald green eyes twinkling beneath a wispy fringe of flaxen hair as she laughingly pointed to herself to add, 'Oh, I'm Annabella… And usually my tummy spins for a few weeks.'

But when, like Kat had done, she twisted slightly to look at the occupant of the next couch, Annabella found herself gazing into the round, blue eyes of a hunched over man who scowled ferociously at her across the small expanse of floorboards that divided their two settees.

Taken aback by his angry continence, she took several deep breaths as she fought down the childish urge to poke out her tongue.

'Good sir, your face is familiar, yet I can't remember what to call you, which is?'

Reckon he'd be a bit of stud muffin if he smiled... That's if he ever does, Annabella reluctantly thought.

Allowing a mere handful of seconds to speed by while she admired his fiery red beard and the rest of the man's long ashen face. She was then forced to repeat her earlier words when only a drawn-out silence greeted her politely posed question.

Even though, he found it hard to decipher the strange dialect of the three women, nevertheless gleaned enough to know a response was required, the man blinked owlishly whilst fervently praying, *Lord, Jesus, Mother, Mary and Moses help me. 'Cause ye must ken, I swear I dinna know what the hell 'tis going on.*

If the style of his clothing had left any doubt about the nationality of the man, his strong Scottish accent didn't when he by-passed Annabella to bark at Michaela, 'I'm James Rory McGregor but 'tis Mac I answer to… And I dinna understand what the hell ye are on about ye silly lass. The last thing I remember 'twas sitting around the fire with me wife and clan after supper.'

One hand curled and uncurled around the hilt of the weapon strapped to his slim waist as the Scotsman squared his shoulders and flung the other up into the air. The swift upward motion exposing previously hidden blood stains which had coated the lower half of his bleached shirt before running in a myriad of rivulets down to congeal in a reddish brownish pool at the hem of his woollen kilt.

Armed, smelly, bloody and rude. What the bejeezers is going on here, Bro? Michaela grumped.

Warily eyeing the Scotsman's weapon and clothing. The tiny woman gave William's hand a warning squeeze, then with just a hint of impatience skimming through her vocal cords

16

replied, 'As I said Mac, we've moved plains. Your memories haven't kicked in that's all... Okay?'

'Nay 'tis not all right, iffen that 'tis what ye are a meaning Missy. I nay understand what ye are on about but my mind's fine and I dinna recall any of ye,' Mac sharply refuted. 'Nay do I recall clapping me sight on this place afore.'

No longer able to keep his head from dropping between bare, knobbed knees, the distraught man stared morosely at his fur bound feet desperately wanting a jug of the whiskey which would normally be the reason he felt so ill.

None appeared ta have weapons. Thus it would nowt be a problem ta take 'em, he tried to reassure himself. *And 'tis stranger still, that nowt but the wee woman is attired in any kind of clothing I recognise.*

Feeling his face redden when he glanced at Annabella's low-cut tee-shirt, whose snug fit displayed her ample breasts to perfection, his father often voiced, '' Tis best to use ye brain first then only iffen that fails, ye brawn laddie,' rose from the foggy depths of his brain.

As the mantra swirled out in ever-widening circles until there was room for no other thought bar this in his head, Mac flicked a finger at the young man lounging nonchalantly, nonetheless fully alert, against the armrest of the last couch.

Wide shouldered and slim of build, the youth had short brown hair and large bluish-green eyes. Rather, scruffily attired in a stained and torn light blue tee shirt, an equally disreputable pair of navy track pants ended an inch or so above the ankle bone of his long legs.

'Mac, everyone. I'm Jank de Sir and like it appears to be for the majority of us, the twentieth century was also my original plain,' he quietly stated before propping his unshaven

17

chin in one hand and directing a snappy salute towards William along with a cheekier. 'You awake over there, old man?'

Acknowledging his eldest child with a small dip of his head William replied, 'Hello it's nice to see you all again. In case you're yet to recall me, I'm William and Michaela's soulmate.'

William's light tenor was nearly overpowered by the loud explosion of sparks which suddenly shot from the fireplace. But since most of the glowing embers landed on the stone hearth, and the rest died before they could scar the glossy floor, he turned his attention back to the problem of the sallow faced Scot.

'Mickey love, what's going on... Why doesn't Mac understand he's dead?'

Sympathy washed over Michaela's face when she saw the same dark question reflected in the Scotsman's disbelieving eyes. Her joy at being reunited with her family and dearest friend somewhat diminished by the anomaly of his death.

Fine kettle of fish this is, Bro. How on earth does a new soul happen to start out on a working plain, eh Master? The least you could do for the poor man is to give me an answer to that one.

Persisting with her noiseless objections. The tiny woman straightened her taut shoulders before standing up and walking back over to Mac's divan.

'May I?' Without giving him time to neither decline or accept, Michaela sat down and reached for his blood smeared hand. The tension radiating off the bewildered man visibly heightened at her touch but encouraged by the fact he made no move to shrug it off she said, 'Mac you've died and passed

18

over. Why it's been done like this I have no answer for… I was given a list of to do's and how to do it's. Alas none gave an iota of reference to your particular situation.'

Mac had long thought himself as quick of mind as of sword. Thus his inability to comprehend the nuances of the wee woman's conversation saw his accent broaden with every word spoken.

'Ye're a blathering woman, so I say again,' he cried. 'One minute, I'm a sitting around the campfire with me wife and clan, tha' next I'm here.'

This said, Mac freed himself from Michaela's tentative touch and in a flurry of angry movement leapt from the couch. Stomping over to squat down in front of the fireplace he thrust his trembling hands over the fire's gambolling flames in a vain attempt to put some warmth back into his shock chilled body.

'I'm sorry,' Michaela sighed. Feeling a bit like an overworked yo-yo, she also stood up and motioning to the remaining four to follow, headed for the furthest end of the chamber. 'Perhaps, there'll be some answers for you tomorrow Mac, but for now how about some food? We'll probably all do better with some nourishment in our stomachs.'

It was more the variety of noises their differently styled footwear made on the bare floorboards than Michaela's sombre, matter of fact tone which saw Mac spin round in time to watch them obey her noiseless gesture. Not by nature an indecisive man, he found himself torn. Both unwilling to believe what he understood Michaela to have said and the irrefutable evidence of his own eyes.

Julz me sweet Irish rose, the old witch ye call Ma never saw this in the sheep's guts she was so fond of dabbling in. This canna be nought but a pile of shite, and I'll soon awake to the comfort of ye soft arms.

Unsteadily getting to his feet whilst clinging to the picture which accompanied these wishful notions, the Scotsman slowly shuffled over to the table. His innate courteously seeing Kat comfortably seated before he slumped into the empty chair between Jank and the pretty blond.

'What's for dinner?' An intrigued Annabella asked as she looked over the table that, with the exception of a crystal candelabra neatly positioned in its centre, was empty.

'Aha, this I do have an answer for,' Michaela chuckled. 'Simply visualize the food you want to eat and it will appear in front of you.'

Once again unable to give any credence to Michaela's words, Mac thumped both of his fisted hands down on the tabletop as he yelled a frustrated, 'Ye Gods… Ye're truly are off ye head, ye wee daft lass.'

Glancing around the table as she gritted her teeth instead of replying straightaway to his curt outburst. Michaela directed a sharply pointed look at her husband and son, who both seemed quite ready and willing to throttle the man, then nodded towards the candelabra's unlit candles.

'No, actually I'm not. It's really quite easy,' she coolly retorted. 'Here try some of this.'

When a small loaf of sour dough bread, knife, side plate and a pot of creamy butter materialised to the left of each person. The aroma of freshly baked bread intertwined with the subtle scent of sandalwood which drifted out from the now lit candles.

'Whatever you want… Just think of it and it will appear. Or perhaps, something to clean our hands with would be in order… Unless you'd prefer a shower prior to dinner, Mac?'

In two minds as to whether she should mention the state of his clothes and unpleasant body odour, Michaela was glad she wasn't sitting next to him when the dishevelled man brusquely shook his head. And although the ancient adage, 'Have doubt, do nowt,' stayed the urge to douse him in hot soapy water. Michaela produced a bottle of hand sanitizer and slid it across the table.

Yet when another look of frustrated anger added more splotches of scarlet to Mac's already glowing face, Jank intercepted the container.

'Doubt he's got the foggiest idea of what to do with this, so shall I go first?' he asked with friendly sarcasm.

Smirking at Michaela's grimaced apology, Jank explained the purpose of the gel he pumped into his own, then the unenthusiastic Scotsman's, hand before passing it around the table.

Annabella had spent numerous decades since her original passing either studying or working within the physical and aloft plains of the eighteenth-century British Isles. So aware most men of that era wouldn't normally refuse the offer of a glass of ale, she successfully materialised a frothing tankard of beer.

'Drink, good sir?' She chirped, yet was forced to produce another then drink from both before Mac wiped the rest of the cleansing gel on the side of his kilt and with just a small twitch of his nostrils, took a wary sip of the overflowing brew.

The flavour must have sat well with his taste buds, Annabella thought, watching Mac empty the tankard in four long gulps and use the back of his freckled hand to muffle a loudish burp after the last.

'Whatever you want, just think of it and it shall appear,'

Michaela grinned. 'Whilst I know this is unusual like Annie so ably showed… It's easy once you get the hang of it.'

'Unusual, yep that's it,' Kat giggled as a plate of sushi and a pot of green tea appeared on the table before her. 'Mickey you sure do believe in understating things, don't you?'

'Mmm, she sure does,' William murmured. The sight of his own meal of fillet steak slathered with mushroom sauce, accompanied by a pile of golden chips and a small garden salad, changing his naturally stern demeanour to a more relaxed, satisfied grin.

Having watched the different varieties of food appear, most of which he failed to recognise, Mac closed his eyes and uttered up a pleading, *Oh, dear Lord help me… 'Tis more magic,* then opened them again to mumble a confused, 'I canna make up my mind.'

'Here have some of this,' Annabella offered, holding out the large bowl of salad she'd chosen to eat.

Screwing up his nose, Mac shuddered distastefully as he viewed the inoffensive greens.

'Nay, thanks lass, I dinna eat grass unless there's nowt else.'

Not understanding the amused reaction to his blunt refusal, for he'd no trouble remembering the adverse circumstances of his early childhood which had seen him do just that, Mac blinked and frowned.

Thudding onto the tabletop the instant his auburn brows met in the centre of his forehead, the steamy aroma of roasting lamb overrode all others while a platter of jacket potatoes dripping with butter, a huge pottery bowl piled high with strawberries and clotted cream, swiftly followed by several more tankards of ale, filled what little space remained in front

22

of the Scotsman.

By tactic agreement their mealtime conversation had been kept to catching up with the news from their former plains. But eying the multitude of empty dishes covering the table's smooth surface, William decided a more serious discussion was well overdue.

'Question and answer time Mickey,' he said. 'Do you know why our passing on has been done like this or where we actually are?'

'Ohh sorry… No answers to the why nor where we are at the present time. I do know we've all been chosen to initiate the colonisation of a new plain,' Michaela replied. 'Like you did, I initially awoke on a daybed similar to yours. Two purple robed figures were sitting in chairs which floated several feet above the floor, yet I felt nothing but peace and calm. To be truthful, I can't ever remember feeling so safe unless you were with me.'

Or you, dear Boss, she soundlessly added. Her earlier displeasure with their Master forgotten as the warmth of the moment once again swept over her.

Red dots of anger tinted his sharp cheek bones as William picked up Michaela's hand from where it rested in her lap. Raising it to his lips he muttered, 'Wish I'd been with you.'

Michaela hadn't always appreciated her man's protective side. Chivalrous in intent though it nearly always was, there'd been the odd occasion when his input had only made things worse than they'd already been. Though not this time, the clasp of his hand sorely missed until the soothing emotions of the unknown room she'd awoken in had taken over.

Shrugging off the remnants of her momentary fright with

23

a toss of her long dark hair, Michaela laughed, 'I've had far less pleasant experiences than that dear one… The woman spoke first saying that if I would freely help you become aware we would all become part of something majestic. Then the man floated a letter over to me and explained the basics… Well mainly the materialising part, and said that when I was ready to leave, I merely needed to think Bro's house. And since they vanished before I could ask anything else I looked about a bit, thought up a few things and ta da, one Bro's house later, there you all were snoring your heads off.'

'Does that mean we're in the Master's place?' Annabella whispered, her eyes filling with amazement as she looked around the room. 'And they really didn't give you any other clues?'

'Er, not necessarily to your first question and kinda to the last. When I consciously think Bro's house again it's supposed to take us back to where I came from. Apparently, they'll be joining us tomorrow. I doubt we were together for more than five minutes.' Allowing her eyes to wander between William and Annabella, Michaela shrugged her shoulders again whilst adding a puzzled, slightly annoyed, 'I don't know what all the theatrics were about. The woman was Jannelle, 'cause I'd recognise her voice anywhere and I bet my next cappa her co-conspirator was Bustie… Because he was absolutely humongous.'

'You didn't get a look at their faces?' Kat quizzed as she tried to remember if she should know the people her aunt referred to.

'Nah, didn't get closer than five feet if that… And they had their cowls up all the time.'

As the faces of the souls Michaela spoke about swam in

24

front of his inner eye, Jank grunted, 'Oh, those two? And so what, everything we want or need to do will be that easy?'

'Somehow, I don't really think that'll be the case. Although everything worked at dinner, didn't it? We thought food and there it was. One minute, I was in the suite of rooms, then one Bro's house and I don't know how long later, I ended up here.'

Squirming in her seat when a shudder of trepidation ran over her body Kat said, 'Rather you than me. It's pretty weird stuff even if you do factor in where we are. Was there anything else?'

'Mmm, I had to place my hand on your foreheads or, in Mac's case, the back of his neck and spout a few words which, I *think*, woke you up,' Michaela replied, removing her dirty dishes with a dismissive thought and brief nod of her head. 'Offer you refreshments and let you know we're expected to participate in an environmental course in the morning. The apartment I first materialised in had two suites of bedrooms and bathrooms attached to the living area. Thus, if everybody's finished, I suggest we clean up and go see if we can't sort a few things out.'

'Does everybody have to think it or only you?' Jank queried once the table was returned to its former pristine state.

Moving his chair back with a harder than necessary shove, Mac growled, 'Aye and 'tis ye thinking enough or do we have ta have contact with each other?'

'Well, I don't know. But if we circle up at least we'll be in touch with each other,' Michaela replied, hoping this would be enough to satisfy the man who'd barely participated in their meal-time conversation, countering any queries directed his way with a distracted, generally curt aye or nay.

While the Scotsman's understanding of the stranger's mode of speaking had increased ten-fold in the past half hour, coming to terms with their tales and the sorcery of the meal he'd been able to produce was another matter. Nor was he able to find it within himself to trust the expression of open honesty that had settled on Michaela's small, pointed face.

'Sooo ye dinna know a lot more than us, do ye lass,' he snorted into the thought filled silence that had fallen over the group.

'I can't help that. You've got all the information I was given,' Michaela muttered, then canted her head back to peer up into the cantankerous man's eyes while she added a soft yet firm. 'I'd recommend some contact... It *was* pretty scary on my own.'

'Aye well scary or nay, 'tis nowt much,' Mac scoffed as he spun away from the people so tolerant of the strange mores they'd awoken too, to put as much distance between them that the dimensions of the chamber would allow.

'Let me,' Annabella whispered when Michaela moved to follow.

Gliding to a standstill beside Mac, Annabella cautiously placed one scarlet tipped finger on his rigid back and said, 'Mac, this is strange to everyone not only you.'

'Odd ta all? How do ye know lass? Just because ye mayhap remember them, dinna mean they're righteous...' Pausing to cast a fleeting glance her way before returning his gaze to the wall he'd been staring at Mac baldly stated, 'I've learnt and me creed is... Trust no one until they have proven themselves trustworthy.'

'I think you'll find they are... Your sentiment may have been required in the era of your physical plain yet up here souls think the other way around or remain under the watchful eyes of the Assessors. This may not be the normal way things are done aloft nevertheless I feel quite at ease here... Besides,' Annabella laughed, pointing to the animal skin pouch attached to his belt. 'By the looks of things there's no other way out of here unless you have a chainsaw in your sporran.'

Finally allowing himself to look down into her twinkling eyes Mac mumbled, 'Nay chain nor saw lassie.'

'In that case…'

'Nay case either,' and as he watched the upward curve of her crimson mouth widen even further Mac added a sincere, 'I'm sorry iffen I've been a bit rude or crass lass, but 'tis all so terribly hard ta believe.'

Encouraged by the effort he was obviously making to control his emotions, and mindful of her own initial passing, and how long it had taken her to fully comprehend what had occurred, Annabella extended her elbow with a jaunty, 'Thus my wee laddie, prudence suggests it's mayhap better to be with company than alone, does it not?'

'Aye mayhap it 'tis,' Mac said, a twinge of a smile crossing his long face as he slipped his hand through the bow in her arm and escorted her back to the table.

Having taken offence at the way the man had again spoken to his wife. William glared at Mac and refusing to clothe his displeasure in anything kinder demanded, 'Are you coming or not?'

'Aye I am.'

Without reacting to her soulmate's mumbled response, Michaela watched the last of their hands connect before closing her eyes and with just a drop of apprehension thought, *Bro's house.*

The sudden jolt of her feet touching something solid forced Michaela to ignore a once more roiling belly and squint through slowly opening eyelashes. 'Phew, it worked.'

The pleased relief that had skipped through her soft exclamation caused a ripple of laughter to break out. But as William stared across the circle to where Mac stood rocking back and forth, the man's strained face and wild eyes compelled him to reluctantly inquire, 'You okay, mate?'

'I'm bonny, 'tis nowt ta fret ye self about,' Mac muttered around a tongue loaded with lumpy bile.

Hearing this, both of William's eyebrows shot skywards, his facial muscles adding to their air of blatant disbelief while Kat quickly laughed, 'Um, I think I ate too much… Mickey, where's the bathroom?'

'I don't think it matters who goes where. Thus, if the ladies have that one…' Michaela was just as quick to reply. The grateful look his soulmate gave Kat wasn't missed by William. Nor was the one of warning that replaced it before she swung an arm towards the ornately scrolled wooden door behind the girl then the matching one opposite it. 'You guys can have the other.'

Lowering his head from studying the murals painted on the arched ceiling Jank said, 'Twenty minutes enough?'

'More than,' Michaela agreed as she stood on tip toe to whisper against William's ear.

William's own original passing hadn't been without its downside. For though he'd been given numerous opportunities to watch over his family and friends' earthly doings, their separation left an ache which even the most pleasurable

28

moments aloft couldn't completely alleviate. Still, compared to the oddity of the Scotsman's it had been far less traumatic. So while they watched the women disappear into their allotted rooms, he scoured his brain for a topic that wouldn't set the twitchy Scot's temper ablaze.

The awkward silence growing until he gave up and held out his hand with a less than titillating, 'I'm William... What area of Scotland do you come from, Mac?'

'Clan Chieftain James Rory McGregor of Loch Side 1822,' Mac answered, giving William's proffered hand a long, hard squeeze. 'Leastways that's where I was born but like I told ye, I dinna answer ta James, 'tis Mac.'

'And I'm Jank de Sir from Tasmania, Australia. Original conception twentieth century,' Jank reiterated.

Rudely brushing aside the younger man's also outstretched arm, Mac reached for his knife.

'I dinna think time travels possible ye wee sprat,' he yelled. 'Ye're all bloody well a lying.'

Twirling the slender stiletto which had appeared in his hand long before Mac finished speaking with confident ease Jank mocked, 'I know for certain that it is ye wee sprat and now so do you. Ye're bloody well a lying.'

An inch was all that separated the two in height, however Mac would have at least twenty kilos on Jank, William judged. The fact that neither had yet moved to engage the other keeping him motionless.

And less than a heartbeat later his cautious insight was rewarded as Mac took a few backward steps whilst snarling, 'I could take ye quicker than ye would ever think possible, but ye are fine for now... I dinna fight with wee children.'

Then thrusting his knife back into its sheath Mac reversed his footsteps, and with arrogant disregard for Jank's glittering blade repeated the latter part of his sentence. Each word accompanied by a sharp nod of his fiery, red head.

Raising nothing more than a disdainful eyebrow. Jank remained motionless as Mac leant forward until their noses almost met to hiss a last threatening, 'And ye be glad of it boy,' before striding over to the door of the second suite.

'It slides across,' William blandly informed the man, but only after the irate Scot began to pound the wall with the heel of one hand while the palm of the other continued to roam over the panelled door searching for the means to open it.

Whether the upward tilt of Mac's chin was one of thanks or not wasn't easy to read. But it was most likely the latter, William decided, when the Scotsman eventually managed to slide the door open, then stomped into the room beyond before banging it shut behind him.

The tension oozed from his long, well-muscled body as Jank dematerialized his slender blade and sagged against the sidewall of the large, mostly empty sitting room.

'Geez he's a bloody worry.'

'You were pretty cool-headed just now,' William praised. 'Though so you should be since this is your what? Hundred and ninety-ninth passing?'

'Thanks, and actually it's my two-hundredth.'

'Sorry must have missed one. Wish we knew what's going on with our, er, upset companion. Someone's certainly stuffed up.'

'Yeah, he's had a damned weird first entry, poor bastard. Have you known him before?'

'Not as Mac. Though thanks to a heads up from your mum, I'm relatively sure he's a friend from the era of our original departure.'

'In that case I suppose we should go see how he is.'

'Mandatory Social Behaviour 101.' The memory of Michaela's departing comment causing William to add a wry, 'Else you know who, will use our guts for gizzard stew.'

When Jank accessed the door Mac had slammed so loudly, they found him standing in front of a long, bevelled mirror, frantically rubbing at the bloodstains on his shirt.

'Ye could have told me how bad I looked,' he grumbled, giving up on the telling smears to spread his arms out. 'Me wife wouldn't be happy I ate with the lassies looking like this.'

'Tough, it's too late now and they had plenty of time to say something if they were truly offended,' William said, acknowledging the fretful apology in the man's eyes with a brief smile. 'I think we should get you cleaned up and mayhap into something more appropriate, don't you?'

'Aye, thank ye, I dinna think of that,' Mac nodded, his eyes locking onto Jank's reflection in the mirror as he bluntly announced, 'I was reputedly one of the best knifemen in Scotland laddie. Thus tha' next time ye decide to lie to me… Ye be prepared for a wee fight.'

This time William did step between the two. Holding up a reproving hand he drawled an exasperated, 'He's not, and nobody is, lying.'

'Then his brains are addled. 'Tis the eighteenth-century nay what the young fool said.'

'Jank's neither liar nor fool… And I can personally attest to his birth date,' William firmly emphasized. 'But regardless of what era we all come from, if he's actually five years younger than you at the present I'll be very surprised.'

Mac's eyebrows shrank into another line across his forehead as he slowly turned to glower at Jank over William's shoulder. But when his knees suddenly buckled, he found himself collapsing onto the small, wooden stool wedged between the mirror and the corner walls.

'Nay… Nay 'tis all just a wee bad dream and I'll soon awaken.' Yet for all Mac's stubborn procrastinations, there was an inkling of acceptance attached to his then quietly posed, 'Iffen we're dead how come we have ta eat and where are the angels and harps? Or are ye trying to tell me I'm in hell?'

'It's no dream mate… You're dead whether you like it or not, and no you're not in hell,' William assured him. 'Come on cobber let's get you cleaned up so we can get comfortable with the ladies. Perhaps between us we'll be able to make some sense out of it all.'

Regardless of his own view-point, Jank's innate sympathy for the Scotsman saw him bank his simmering temper, and as humour replaced anger think, *Clothes.*

Pulling off the silken green stockings which had suddenly draped themselves around his head, William waved them in front of Mac.

'Mayhap these are more to your liking, good sir?'

'Och mon. I'm no poncy Sassenach laddie but I'll have that wee thing,' and plucking the extra-large linen shirt from the floor, for the first time Mac softly echoed William's laughter as he eyed off the pair of dark green, corduroy trousers that danced beside him. 'Also, these wee things.'

Happy to leave them to it, Jank opened the second door of the small foyer. The short corridor he stepped into had two arched doors moulded into either side of the longer pale cream walls, while the narrower pair's only job was to keep them apart.

Poking his head through one doorway, then nudging the adjacent door open with his foot, he sang out, 'As expected, beds and bathroom this a way.'

But it was his loudly exclaimed, 'Oh crappola,' which saw

William and Mac, laden with clothes and an assortment of toiletries, scurry into the bathroom.

'Okaaay, please note, thinking in the singular not the plural is highly recommended,' Jank advised, chancing a quick glance their way while juggling a multitude of wooden hairbrushes with artful deftness before a sharp click of fingers, and silent vamoose, dispensed with them all.

'Methinks even ye folk have a wee bit ta learn.'

Even though he doubted he'd be shot for doing otherwise, Jank shook the hand Mac extended. Any adverse thoughts he might have kept to himself as the large Scot released his grip and moved further into the bathroom.

Rapidly discarding his knife belt, blood-stained clothing and footwear Mac leant over the sunken bathtub. Stumped by the numerous circles of chrome, his eyes darted between the empty tub and the glass wrapped cubicle next to it.

'I dinna understand, there's nowt pump.'

'Ah but there is,' Jank smirked. 'I'm at your service, your nakedness. Thus, I shall endeavour to explain the whole enchilada.'

'In that case, he's all yours,' William yelled over the music that blared out as Mac's natural inquisitiveness overcame his reluctance to be there, and he began to fiddle with the shiny knobs of the shower recess.

Far longer than anticipated Jank's tuneful, 'We're back,' announced the return of the pair to the outer room.

A wide grin spreading across the younger man's face as he moved beyond the reach of Mac's long arms to lightly guffaw, 'We would've been done way sooner except his Lordship had a problem with the zipper on his pants and refused to let me help him.'

ON PLAIN: BACK WITH THE GIRLS

Positive that their Master would be somewhere about, a hopeful Michaela once again perused the chamber the six souls had previously materialised in. But since only an ash whitened cobweb dangling above the chamber's free standing fireplace was to be seen, a frustrated groan escaped from between her pursed lips.

Walking up behind her in time to hear the faint sound, William placed an arm around Michaela's waist.

His gentle squeeze was accompanied by a knowing, 'Ah, the Boss still isn't speaking, and if we want anything to sit on it's up to us to produce it?'

'Carefully,' Jank advised as he too, came to a halt beside the tiny woman. Another crisply duplicated, *Vamoose,* and flick of fingers removing the swarm of unwanted hairbrushes that had glued themselves to his unguarded memory.

'Ohhh, you seem to have worked that one out,' Michaela grinned up at him.

'Well almost,' Jank replied with a self-deprecating laugh. 'Almost.'

'If when you decide to materialise things, you need to think… And if thinking itself materialises your thoughts what comes first?' A bewildered Annabella questioned. 'Apart from the ale I simply thought salad at dinnertime.'

'Errr yeah good point,' Jank shrugged. 'I suggest we need to clear our minds then concentrate on producing only one piece of furniture. Therefore, on the count of three…'

Four chairs, one couch and a deer hide wrapped stool arrived to hover at waist height behind each soul as the room erupted in a zing of displaced air. The series of dull thuds each piece made when connecting with the floorboards was partly muffled by a square of woollen carpet that a quick-witted William had slipped between their feet and those of the newly arrived furnishings.

'Wow, this place really is the bee's knees,' Kat cried, flinging herself backwards into the plump lounge chair she'd conjured up and pressing its side button to activate the footrest.

Snuggling into the comfort of her own seat Michaela produced a small glass table closely followed by several steaming mugs.

'Indeed, it is,' she grinned. 'Coffee anyone? And at this point we know exactly what?'

'Foods good…'

'Boring décor…'

'Yes please, and we've passed on again…'

'Bugger all…'

He'd remained silent as the volley of words clambered to be heard over one another yet when the tittered reaction to Jank's mild swearing died down Mac couldn't refrain from crying, 'I canna understand this dying business for I dinna feel dead.'

'Jeez mate, get over it,' Jank forcefully demanded. 'Like it or nay, you're dead.'

Unsure of what might've happened whilst they'd been apart, Michaela cast a worried glance between the two. And though Mac didn't seem at all put out by Jank's gruff tone nor the bluntness of his wording murmured a much kinder, 'It can

35

be extremely hard for some people to comprehend, Mac, but when you die your soul passes on.'

'Whist wee one I'm a believer... So ye must understand the Holy One and his teachings are always within my heart.'

'Us too, for obviously it goes with the territory,' Michaela nodded. 'Still, the lifestyle you chose to adopt on your previous or original plain does impact on the length of time it takes to atone for sins still outstanding at the time of your demise or departure. It can also influence personal off plain visitation requests, the type of community service you're given and any additional tasks you might be called on to undertake once residing on a working plain.'

'Och woman, whilst I dinna quite ken ye last bit of business if ye are a God loving person ye should repent ye errors afore ye die.'

Restlessly tapping her fingers up and down Kat broke in with a terse, 'Any intelligent person knows some never want nor see the need to do so... Besides what about those who simply don't have the opportunity to rectify their circumstances?'

Casting an appreciative nonetheless disapproving glance at the shapely expanse of tanned legs showcased by the brevity of Kat's denim shorts, which he felt sure no decent woman of his clan would ever have dreamed of displaying publicly, Mac snapped, 'I believe God knows what's what with his good ones and tha' others go straight ta hell.'

'Not necessarily,' Kat rebutted. 'There's some conjecture whether a Hell even exists below the Lower Punishment Plain.'

'Bollocks, lass, I dinna ken about ye other, but of course, there's a Hell. I've sent many a slimy creature there me self.'

36

The footrest on Kat's chair collapsed with a loud clunk as she sat upright then leant forward to scathingly condemn, 'Proud of that are you?'

'Nay I'm not, but dinna think I'm overly perturbed either… They were right bastards, each and every one of them,' Mac fired back with well-deserved confidence. The multiple times he'd been charged with defending his actions in the halls of Scotland's highest courts having at least seen him savour the sweet justification of victory, if not much else.

Absolutely certain there would be ample time in the coming decades for the pair to debate the subject as much as they cared too, Michaela put out her hand to stay Kat's reply as her mind tried to sort out a way to explain the dying process in language Mac could fathom or wouldn't be confused by.

'After your original passing, then normally every subsequent one thereafter, your soul is re-directed to the Assessment Plain. There, your actions on the physical plain are assessed, and if deemed worthy, you undertake training in any of the Humanitarian areas the Assessment Panel may require you to round out. You usually get to choose the era of your working plain and mayhap the roll you'll undertake there. On arrival at each one, you participate in a mandatory Induction Course which should cover the period of history the plain itself spans, its environment and charter.'

'And each…' William said, indicating to Michaela to take a sip of her cooling drink while he explained the final salient details. '…Soul may apply to move plains and most eventually do. Mickey and I are soul mated and we've both just celebrated our three-hundredth passing. This means we've been sent back two hundred and ninety-nine times to live out a life span, or part thereof, depending on the requirements of the mission.

37

This is Jank's two hundredth. Ladies what about you?'

'The same,' Kat and Annabella replied in unison.

With accent thickening and head swivelling from side-to-side Mac blankly stated, 'By rights ye remember it, this first passing on? Plus, ye others. Thus, I canna have done it before 'cause I think I would remember dying… And I tell ye straight even in my wildest dreams, this 'tis nay what I expected.'

'Generally speaking, if you've been here before you remember everything once you're aloft for a little bit, if not immediately,' Annabella told him, the hand she ran over his hunched shoulders offering more comfort than she realised. 'The Archival mandate clearly states you need to know where you've come from and what you experienced there.'

'Aye well, I dinna think remembering's me problem and I'd like to think I would've done it a wee bit better than this,' Mac replied with a condescending sniff.

'Mac this is not the way it's supposed to be done,' Michaela apologised, the wry curl of her lips and elevation of one dark eyebrow a visible precursor to the irony of her next words. 'As said, prior to your arrival, it was our understanding that after an initial, if not every, passing a soul must go to the Assessment Arches before traveling elsewhere.'

'I still dinna understand ye missy… And nowt of ye speak with any accent I'm familiar with.'

'Well, no we wouldn't, and that's why this or rather your case is so, um, unusual,' Michaela began. 'The Archivist…'

'Do I have ta repeat every bloody thing lass? Who or what is a bloody Archivist?'

Though Mac's temper threatened to override him again he was still mindful of Annabella's soft, warm hand. Carefully reaching around to remove it from his back before rising to pace back and forth across room.

'Sod it Mac, calm down and we'll explain some more. But dammit keep in mind it's neither Mum's fault… Nor Kat's, nor anyone else in the room which probably includes yourself. So kindly do us a favour and just accept it as a given,' Jank bellowed. 'You've learnt or been told enough to know we didn't put you here.'

Returning to where his stool was as a torrent of rapid sentences flew from between his chattering teeth Mac said, 'Hell's bells I'm a sorry everyone, and aye lad that ye have. I… I dinna remember the last time I've had to ask for forgiveness so often, yet those who deal with me consider me ta be a fair man. Thus, if ye dinna mind young Kat, I'll copy ye chair and get comfortable again. Then ye can perhaps tell me about your um, Inductions. I canna help thinking some colour ta your tales mayhap be of some aid ta me.'

Into the short silence which followed Mac's seemingly sincere words of contrition came the now familiar whooshing sound as his stool vanished and a red leather lounge chair took its place.

'Mmm, if we are going to tell stories I need more food. All this mind mumbling makes me ravenous,' Annabella said, idea instantly becoming deed as a steaming platter of king prawns, crumbed calamari and dipping sauces materialised in her outstretched hand.

Pleased to see the tension which so often seemed to seep from every pore of Mac's skin once again dissolve. William plucked an octopus ring from the plate with a laughing, 'Love your thinking Annie… And another drink anyone? My shout.'

'Bloody hell,' Mac swore. 'Do we have ta pay for this or perhaps work it off?'

'Eat, drink,' Jank replied. '… And listen.'

Wondering if they'd come from the cool waters surrounding her home state as Tasmania's seafood had been, and no doubt still was, considered amongst the best on the planet Annabella gave Mac a brief description of the food she'd produced.

'You don't need to work to eat or have a roof over your head,' Michaela said, referring back to Mac's question after Annabella had ceased speaking and he'd gingerly taken one of each from the glass platter. 'But if you can't follow what we say, feel free to interrupt.'

ON PLAIN: FOUNDERS INDUCTION DAY

Jank opened his eyes as the early morning light began to creep through the room's one small, slightly ajar window. Rising from his bed, he edged past a lightly snoring William and stood before the casement admiring what he could see of the distant snow-capped mountains.

Alerted by the small snick of the door latch, he turned in time to watch the bare-chested Scot, hips swathed in white towelling, head for his rumpled bed.

'Nay, I didn't, but good morn to you laddie,' Mac said in response to Jank's mild greeting, his weary reply a sharp contrast to the cheerful sounds of Wattle birds nattering to each other as they flew past the lace draped window.

'Ditto, and me next,' Jank said, nodding towards the bathroom door. 'Once Dad's up we can see if the girls are awake.'

'I heard a wee noise afore I washed so 'tis likely they await us in the other room already... What do ye think we should wear today? Mind, 'tis not a question I would normally ask ye ken. Just until I know what's what I'd appreciate some guidance.'

Waking as Mac's quiet burr penetrated his slumbers, William flung back his doona.

'Morning all and comfortable mate,' he recommended, rising to stretch his arms out wide. 'Here try these.'

'You've got to be kidding, Willie.' With a grimace of

distaste Jank grabbed the closest pillow. Welding it like a cricket bat he deflected one after the other of the offending line of clothing marching towards him as he added, 'I'm so not wearing that stuff.'

'Why? It's probably the most practical and safest you'll find on any plain irrespective of your personal tastes. And since I'm not your great-grandfather it's Dad, Will or William,' William retorted. 'Do you want to use the facilities first?'

'Nah you go, and I wore the wretched things for like a solid ten freaking years,' Jank complained before sending the final ball of socks flying through the air.

Deftly deflecting the well-aimed projectile so it thudded against the side wall instead of his nose, William asked if that meant Jank had been aloft during what was commonly known as the Glitch era.

'Yeah, my original entry was fair bung in the middle of it and I covered the basics of that with Mac last night, oh Forgetful one,' Jank said, boosting his taunt with a pointed, 'I'd have thought that's one date you'd never forget considering the kerfuffle you and Mum made at the time.'

Whatever William's reply may have been it wasn't heard, overshadowed by Mac's loudly rumbling stomach which easily reached across the room to where the man now leant against the bathroom door.

'Aye briefly laddie but then ye got onto the English and History discs and I dinna think we got back to the topic,' Mac clarified around a cluster of deep belches. 'Iffen ye and Jank get ta doing ye ablutions we can think about filling our bellies.'

'If you're really that hungry you could always conjure something up cobber,' Jank reminded him as William moved to do Mac's bidding and he was left watching the rather

42

complex man begin to confine his damp hair in a series of thick braids.

'Aye but 'tis nice eating together, dinna ye think?'

Five minutes later, a loud knocking on their bedroom door and an equally robust, 'Are you lot decent?'

Preceded the blond, ponytailed head that popped around the opening door.

'Good morning, breakfast's up.'

Kat's cheery salutation was swiftly followed by an, 'Ooops sorry,' as her eyes swept over the mostly naked body sitting on the bed nearest to where she stood.

Undaunted by what she saw the petite girl blatantly eyed Mac up and down, emitted a pert wolf whistle, and made a giggling departure when Jank replied that they'd all be there soon.

Re-entering the bedroom only moments after the outer door clicked shut again, William said, 'Suits you, Mac.'

Still sitting on his rumpled bed, but now clad in dark green cargo pants and a close-fitting rugby top, Mac tugged the matching beanie from his head and ran a large, freckled finger over the emblem sewn into the front of it.

'Aye well,' he murmured. 'The laddie could've been a bit quicker with his thinking for the wee blond lassie mayhap be a fretted by me nakedness.'

'Oooh, I don't think so. It would take more than your hairless chest to worry Kat,' Jank snickered. 'Besides you're the one who was so mortified not her. The look on your face said it all mate, it truly did.'

Quick to pick up the thread of their conversation. William ignored both Mac's reddening face and the fact that Jank no longer wore the tee-shirt and boxer shorts he'd worn to sleep in to ask, 'Would you like us to wait for you Jank?'

'Nup,' Jank responded with a self-satisfied chuckle. 'I've already thought myself clean.'

'Aye, dressed anyways,' Mac said, bending towards the younger man to sniff the air around him. 'But he nowt stinks thus methinks his magic mayhap worked.'

Eager for the day's events to begin. The six had already broken their fast and were now amidst a lively debate about what to do next when Mac's voice rose above the rest.

'Och my dear sweet ladies, surely a wee walk won't hurt ye.'

Not remotely interested in climbing the distant range of snow blanketed mountains which appeared to be the main focus of the men's desire to explore. Annabella replied with an even louder and unfortunately truthful, 'Come on Mac, you know we can't 'cause we don't know what time we'll be summoned.'

'Their problem. They should've given us a time-table,' Jank shrugged. 'Let's try thinking ourselves there and see what happens?'

A trio of very loud 'No's,' followed the younger man's remark yet before the discussion could roll any further three, two-seater couches appeared. Kept to a consistent height of twelve inches above the cherry-red floorboards, they formed an angled horseshoe across the room.

Comfortable enough looking and covered with a pleasing light mauve leather, the puffed side arms of the outer couches effectively blocked both doorways and left only a singular, extremely narrow, window as an unlikely escape exit.

Which by the worried expressions everyone now wore

they'd all thought of using, then just as swiftly discarded. Leaving just their inner well of faith, and the scant knowledge they'd been privy to, to draw on if things suddenly went astray.

It was the scrape of Jank's chair being pushed back which finally broke the long seconds of silence that had settled over the group. The tall lad standing up and taking a step away from the table as he drolly stated, 'Moot point ladies. Seems like that decision has already been made for methinks Boot Camp 101 is about to start.'

The deep bow and out flung arm that followed was a noiseless request for the five to precede him. Yet needed his challenging, 'Snap out of it, people, our future awaits... All aboard the float divans, destination unknown,' Jank then added for the remaining chairs to be hastily emptied and neatly positioned back under the table.

Startled by the harnesses that flowed out from invisible sockets as soon as his bottom touched the soft material of the couch, Jank's sigh of surprise mingled with those of his companions. Coming together in the design of a cross, the safety restraints clipped together at the centre of each stomach while footrests sprang out to support their feet. And when the outer arms of the two external couches moved inward, the triangle they made began to spin round and round, faster and faster.

'Flopping oath,' Annabella cried. 'This's worse than a Gee Whiz.'

'A what, wee one?'

'Umm, it's a carnival ride we have at what your period of time would've called Fair's or Market days. Wouldn't you have been to some of those?'

'Oh aye, of a kind... Nowt had things like this though and

45

iffen it dinna stop soon I mayhap lose me breakfast,' Mac grumbled, his hand darting out to grasp Annabella's as the speed of the rotating seats continued to accelerate.

The sound of Kat's screams of laugher brought a small upward curve to Michaela's mouth but her lips then tightened into a concerned line when she felt a shudder run over William's body.

Looking up in time to see what colour his naturally pale face possessed drain away, she leant sideways as far as the harness allowed to whisper, 'Will, you hanging in there, my love?'

'Not for much longer,' William replied, finding some release for his growing anger as he elevated his voice to yell at the unknown persons driving the couches. 'I think we're overdue to get off you miserable bastards. If you're planning on getting any work out of us today, you'd better stop this stupid bloody nonsense.'

Whether it was William's words or mere happenstance, the triangle of divans immediately ceased to spin. The ends separating again in time for the occupants to see two figures in purple velvet robes, faces well hidden by the deep recesses of their cowls, materialise along with the duo of chairs which floated like tall sentries behind them.

ON PLAIN: TWO MORE

'Welcome to you all. Michaela did your charges sleep well?'

Unsurprised by the husky voice which uttered these warmly spoken words Michaela stood before answering with a coolly drawled, 'Some did, others not so much.'

'Ah yes, James... I wouldn't have thought he'd sleep terribly well.'

Wondering how they would know it was Mac she'd been mainly worried about Michaela quirked an eyebrow and took her time before saying, 'It's his first passing so there's a lot for him to assimilate.'

'Have you filled him in?'

Gruff criticism hardened his broad accent when Mac chose to ignore what he'd been told about the twosome the previous night to answer her question with an intentionally sharp, 'Aye as best they could. But I dinna think nowt of ye manners woman 'cause as ye can see, I'm just over here.'

'Careful James... You're not a clan Chieftain here you know,' the second of the two warned as he flattened out a very impressive set of shoulders.

'Mac, my name 'tis Mac,' the Scotsman snorted, allowing his ever-ready ire to flare into life whilst he strutted towards the newcomers. 'And I dinna ken that at all.'

Unperturbed by the seventy-odd kilos and at least eighty centimetres the being had on him, Mac drew his arm back and, with all the strength of his own not so inconsiderable bulk, swung his fist towards where he judged the stranger's chin would be.

Without moving, the immense man's simple response was a hiss of indrawn breath and an amused, 'Nada, I don't think so.'

Immobilised by invisible ties, the Scotsman found himself back beside Annabella. His loud curses colouring the air around them as he wriggled and squirmed to no avail.

Holding up a neatly manicured hand when everyone else leapt to their feet. The woman yelled over Mac's vocal outrage, 'Please stay where you are. Bustie let him go. You can play later... Mac kindly be silent.'

A variety of emotions ran over the faces of those looking on yet apart from Michaela's loudly whispered, 'Warned ya it would be them,' none moved as the woman brushed back the hood of her robe.

Short, black hair liberally sprinkled with streaks of ash blond framed the round cheeks of her lightly tanned face. Add intelligent blue eyes, a straight regal nose and wide rosy mouth the woman was a vision of exotic beauty.

Around her slender neck she wore a delicate pewter chain from which hung three strands of equally spaced, barely visible silver. At the end of each length lay a flat oval of gold. The central one engraved with a portrait of a small dog, the other two dainty owls. All nestled just above the full, rounded curve of her bosom, their sapphire eyes sparkling with darts of purple fire with every breath she took.

'You can call me, Jannelle and I'm this plain's Chief Justice,' she announced. 'My friend here is Buster it's Master Archivist.'

Discarding his own cowl with a toss of his woolly head. The immense man strolled over until he was just close enough to hold out his hand.

'If you want, I can show you how to do that.'

Mac eyed the huge Aboriginal's ebony hand but refused to offer his own as he sniggered, 'Mayhap you can, mayhap ye cannot but... I nowt think it necessary you stupid wee git.'

As Buster found himself thrown backwards into one of the chairs floating behind Jannelle. A flamboyant twirl of Mac's finger sent the seat and its cargo of flesh spinning away.

The sound of Buster's chair crashing into the far wall a rumbling background for the Scotsman's smugly taunted, 'See I had the right of it. 'Cause ye dinna need ta teach me that one did ye, ye wee turd.'

Remaining where he had been so casually put, Buster's face creased into a brilliant grin as he joined in with the round of loud clapping William had been more than willing to instigate.

'Even dead lads will be lads, won't they?' Annabella sighed when a corresponding smile eventually stayed on the Scotsman's bearded face.

'Yeah, but although methinks some of us know the pair, it's hardly the time for a pissing contest, is it?' Kat replied. 'I thought for a minute we'd have to take him on.'

Smiling as she listened to the two women's quiet conversation before giving both Mac and Buster, who should've known better, an icy glare, the Chief Justice said, 'Now those overgrown idiots have got that wasted bucket of testosterone out of their system, it's time the Inaugural Induction for the last known plain began.'

Apart from the odd, smothered burble of amusement nothing else was said until Mac released the thought keeping Buster confined and he'd floated back to join them.

'Okay,' Jannelle began. 'On this newly created plain it

will be up to us to decide what we wish to achieve here and how the plain is to be governed. Once our charter is formatted, we'll have the overall plus day to day responsibility for ensuring it works. We'll also be responsible for the normal quota of call outs once we're fully operational with at least one team always on standby for emergencies affiliated with the other plains.'

'Good,' a pleased Kat smiled. 'I wondered if we'd still be required for those.'

With his thick, bushy brows suddenly arcing in arrogant surprise Buster said, 'That's the underpinning oath taken by all who manage to travel past the Assessment Plain, and would've been fully covered before your initial Induction took place would it not?'

'It's been a few centuries since we've done that mate,' William reminded the huge man. 'And for some unknown reason, Mac's skipped that bit.'

'Oh right, not everyone having a memory like mine is the one thing I do tend to forget,' Buster replied. 'It's a pity no one else is as brilliant as I.'

Correctly interpreting the way William felt about the immense man's arrogantly spoken comments Jannelle hurriedly stated, 'You know Bust's got the highest IQ of any person ever known, two hundred and eighty and still counting. He often choses to be bloody socially inept, nonetheless as he so immodestly told you… Brilliant.'

Oblivious to the reception of his last words and his friends not so subtle jibe, Buster nodded vigorously then with boyish enthusiasm exclaimed, 'Mac dear boy as to why you haven't passed over before is a lovely mystery, and one I'll enjoy solving. We were told the founding members had all travelled between the plains.'

''Tis nay been lovely for me ye wee sprat and ye were misinformed weren't ye... And whilst we're on the topic, who told ye what anyway?'

Although she felt not an ounce of sympathy for the irritated expressions which sped across the two newcomers faces Michaela snatched at the excuse it gave her to silently gripe, *Yeah, dammit Bro who told 'em that one... Telling porkies again are we?*

Not I, besides he went from physical to aloft, didn't he? Thus, he has travelled between plains so kindly refrain from swearing at me.

Inwardly grinning at her Master's indignant response. The tiny woman ignored his often-voiced censure, and having spared less than a scant moment savouring the warm glow their mute conversations always invoked regardless of content, gleefully chortled, *Aha, got ya... I knew you'd be somewhere about. If you wouldn't mind putting in a personal appearance it would help Mac immensely.*

In due course little one, in due course.

Confound it, Boss, why not?

Because they say so, Bro gently admonished.

Oh, soooo it's one of those Master, a somewhat mollified Michaela replied. *Yet if you could appear, if only for a little bit...*

But though she felt her Master's touch retreat, leaving the tiny woman's plea for him to stay answered by only a quickly diminishing warmth. It took the content of Mac's next sentences to completely shatter her reverie.

'So, I really am dead thus ye were telling me the truth. Pity that, not that I wanted ta think of ye being liars ye ken but I 'twas still hoping I'd awake from a wee dream. As easy as some things seem ta be here, I'd like ta say goodbye to me

51

family and there's a few chores I need ta help me clan with. Also, ye must surely understand, some personal ones.' Pausing to rub a freckled hand over the fresh scars gouged into the skin centred over his heart. There was nothing but loathing in Mac's hard burr when he grunted a final, 'For iffen it's possible I'd like ta have a few minutes alone with tha' gutless bastard who shot me in the back.'

'If he hasn't already paid the appropriate penalty on the physical plains the Assessors should undertake to see him punished aloft,' Jannelle frowned. 'And many a soul have gone back before entering a working plain... But it's not supposed to happen until after the assessment process.'

''Tis both good and bad news ye impart lassie. For iffen it goes like ye say and I've missed those steps... I'm nay ta see me family again nor hold them?' Mac asked, the last of his words ending in a heart-broken whimper as grief-stricken droplets welled in his eyes.

'No, no not at all... Most likely since you're here you'll probably have the opportunity to do so once we're operational,' Buster said with another of his beaming smiles. 'Anyways, once they're dead you can search the archives and find 'em yourself.'

Cringing at the total lack of empathy in his phrasing, Jannelle told Buster to shut up, before assuring Mac they'd make it a priority.

'Aye well, let's get at it then,' the distraught man sniffed.

'Right. Okay when you're ready, join hands, because we're off to the conference room,' Buster ordered with a brisk change of attitude.

'Nay more spinning mind,' Mac admonished.

Jannelle's denial of fault a faint footnote left to drift around the room as the eight souls vanished.

ON PLAIN: CONFERENCE ROOM

Bereft of doors or windows the hexagonal chamber they'd reappeared in also bore a high arched ceiling. Softly displayed by an intricate candelabra suspended from its central apex. Exposed beams of Tasmanian Oak divided wide sections of plaster board coated with vibrant geometrical shapes while a deep maroon carpet hid the floor and the palest of greens coloured the otherwise unadorned walls.

'Cool, no nausea. Anyone else?' When all bar William grinned their reply, Michaela gave his arm a sympathetic pat then canted her head towards the upper reaches. 'Not sure about the, um, artwork and we're gonna need some furniture.'

Pushed to one side by a gentle influx of cool air, Jank mimicked Michaela's nodding head as he sent her a cheeky grin from across the eight-sided table and chairs which now divided them.

'Are the actions really necessary, Mum?' He teased.

'You just used 'em but maybe... Perhaps... Probably not,' Michaela countered with an off-hand shrug.

Sitting down to open the small, lilac sachet that came with the Huon pine topped table. The tiny woman tore an end from the envelope then stopped to peer from one expectant face to the next.

'In case you might perchance think otherwise, none of this is my doing,' she muttered, waving the ragged side of the envelope in the air before tipping it upside down and giving it a good shake.

Tidy lines of writing filled both sides of the small piece of paper that slipped between its broken sides. Flipping it over and reading as she spoke, Michaela said, 'Welcome… You are now eight and on occasion you will be nine. Your first task is to write the charter for this plain, stay safe… Au revoir.'

'That's it?' William said.

'Yep,' Michaela laughed as she handed him the slip of paper. 'Therefore, if everyone would write down er, let's say five things you consider paramount to the ethos of this plain?'

'Wait a sec, Mickey… What about the "and on occasion you'll be nine", doesn't that perturb you? It surely does me.' Except for another slight shift of Michaela's shoulders, Kat's question was also left for the moment, kept from being answered by the appearance of the brightly striped envelope that now hovered less than a millimetre from the tip of the petite girl's nose. Quick to pluck the newcomer away from her face, with an explosion of air Kat added an equally swift, worry tainted, 'Who? And why?'

'Oh, don't bother sweating on the particulars,' Jannelle retorted. 'There's definitely a familiar, overrated and unsolicited macro management pattern emerging here.'

Though she wondered about the irritated tone which went hand in hand with the Chief Justice's cryptic comment. Kat didn't query it as she carefully extracted a thickish sheet of card stock from the colourful casing. Yet an inkling of understanding birthed itself in her mind as she read aloud it's plainly coined, 'Get to work team… You'll need pen and paper.'

Neatly aligning the parchment, quills and inkpot he'd

54

produced where he wanted them to be. Mac looked up to stare in bewilderment at the sleek, slender boxes which sat before his companions. About to vocalize his puzzlement he was stopped by William's snort of laughter. Then joined him as the man lent behind Michaela's chair and plucked a tiny, golden eyed kitten from the protruding draw of the metal filing cabinet his soulmate had unknowingly produced along with her notebook.

'You only need the computer, babe, get rid of the rest.' Eying the messy collection of paraphernalia arrayed around the tall cupboard with distaste, William added a lightly chiding, 'It doesn't matter what plain we're on, if Mickey's focused on something her workroom always looks like this.'

'No, it doesn't, and you can't send Sophie back. Leastways I presume that's who the kitten is?'

'Yeah, I expect it's her Annie.' The unwanted clutter disappearing as Michaela add a complacent, 'The other stuff doesn't matter. But since I don't know exactly where we are, it's not like I can post her back.'

'No, I don't suppose you can,' William smiled. 'Trust Miss Sophia to suss out we'd need an office, because I certainly wasn't given the chance to pack.'

'Me neither. I'm just glad I arrived with some gear on,' Kat blushed. 'I was in the sauna.'

Unable to work out the reason for Buster's splutter of amusement nor the titters of similar ilk that came from the others. Mac scratched his head then tentatively touched the matte black object sitting in front of Jank.

'Umm, laddie what's this thing?'

'It's a computer. One of a variety of different tools we've been writing with since the latter part of the twentieth century,'

Jank replied, sliding the notebook towards Mac. 'Hang on a sec and I'll show you.'

'No. Mac, either use your paper or link up with Jank… And like Michaela suggested, everyone write down five things you consider to be essential aspects of our Charter. Agreed?'

Giving the Chief Justice a long hard look, Jank crossed his arms and demanded to know who'd died and made her boss.

'Wheest lad… Ye've just spent the past few hours trying ta convince me we're all are. And she's nowt but a wee female, thus leave it for now for ye can sort the lassie out later.'

Bloody morons.

But although she glowered across the table at the handsome pair, Jannelle declined to be baited any further by the challenging glint she saw in the duo's eyes. Tempering her quickly rising temper with a spout of colourful blasphemy which furiously swam inside her skull while she waited the few seconds needed for her notebook to boot up.

Surprised by Jannelle's tight-lipped silence, Michaela also left Mac's quip unaccounted for. Instead, she turned to the immense Aboriginal, who was sensible enough to deadpan his face, and asked whether he should be taking minutes yet.

'Ooops, yeah I probably should be,' the Master Archivist ruefully replied. 'Um rather should've been, though I'm pretty lousy at it aren't I Jannie?'

'Actually, that's not the slightest bit true,' Jannelle denied with a dismissive thrust of her chin. 'You've had plenty of training… He just doesn't like doing it, do you my pretty little piece of Pavlova?'

'Aww come on, you're so much better at it than I. Please, pretty please even,' Buster wheedled.

'Like hell I will. You're more than capable of doing it yourself.'

'Come on cobber, I'm so flaming awful the other plains insist I use an Associate.'

'Bulldust... Like they have any choice, you just palm it off onto them.'

Interrupting their playful stirring with an offer to undertake the task for him, Annabella wasn't surprised when Buster thanked her then hurriedly accepted as a sneaky, decidedly satisfied expression flicked across his face.

Once she was sure everyone had finished, Annabella produced a minute U.S.B. stick and said, 'I'm not the quickest at this part, therefore would someone mind contextualizing our responses for me please?'

'Reckon that'll be me, and I think you'll find the computers are linked Anne,' a confident Jank announced while his hand skated over her keyboard with envious dexterity.

'Mm mmm thanks honey,' Annabella hummed.

However, her tuneful purring came to a skidded standstill when Jank pointed to the screen and she read the sparse synopsis he'd highlighted. Finding it hard to believe, the svelte woman re-read it twice more before slowly moving her eyes to where the immense man sat.

'Master Archivist, unless I'm mistaken this is extremely rare... Because the first word we all put down was Teamwork with a capital T. Then in no particular order... Training, Rostering, Housekeeping or Duty of Care,' and as her astounded gaze ran around the group Annabella whispered, 'All of us.'

'Giggling goanna's Annie, you're a hundred per cent correct,' Buster chuckled. 'Historically it's taken weeks, if not months, or in some cases even years, for a plain's founding members to come to an accord on the basic charter concepts.'

'But it is unanimous,' Jannelle confirmed, having leant over to read their responses for herself. 'We all do agree.'

Hands tapping up and down on the tabletop, an agitated Mac cried, 'I hate ta fret ye but that's nowt what I said.'

'Not exactly the same, nonetheless my interpretation is correct,' Jank grinned, holding up his closed fist. His fingers rising one by one as he went on to add, 'You said Brothers in Arms instead of Teamwork... Self-defence and life itself for Training. Providing food, shelter and protection for your clan covered Duty of Care. Rostering by allowing your people to have adequate time to do their duties and for Housekeeping...'

'Nay lad... I nowt do any of that nonsense, 'tis yon women's work,' Mac broke in with a reproachfully stare. 'And I nowt said I did.'

'No, you didn't. But if you'd be kind enough to let me finish.' As his last digit rose to stand beside the rest, Jank proved his point with a firm, 'You reckon you can definitely come up with some better outhouses or, as we call it, waste product facilities now you've seen what's in use here.'

Annabella had just finished explaining Jank had simply modernised his words when yet another envelope, accompanied by a basket of grapes, appeared in front of William.

Repositioning the fruit into the centre of the table before opening the mauve rectangle, William rapidly perused the nearly transparent sheet of paper, then with a sardonic glance directed solely towards the two newcomers quoted, 'Chief Justice Jannelle and Master Archivist Buster... A tough job well done, thank you. Thou may now disclose any known

58

tasks.'

'Sooo ye were holding out on us weren't ye, ye rotten wee buggers.'

'Give us a break man. We've only been reassigned like fifteen minutes more than anyone else,' Buster hotly rebutted.

'Time can be irrelevant elsewhere aloft, so why not here?' Jank argued. 'And I bet all my deserts for the next year that you know a bloody sight more than the rest of us.'

'Only that Jannelle's been selected to hold the positions of Chief Justice and I'm the Master Archivist,' Buster clarified. 'Mickey and Will are to be our Ambassadors...'

'See,' Mac butted in again. 'Like I told ye, holding out on us.'

'Now we're in for it,' William muttered against his soulmates ear. 'Did you know?'

A shiver of denial ran over Michaela's body but she still managed to laugh when Kat stuck up her thumb at her then told Mac to be quiet so Buster could finish what he was saying.

Flashing her a toothy smile the immense man pursed his thick lips and flapped one ham sized hand towards the scowling Scotsman. 'Like she said, if you'll kindly allow me the floor, we mayhap get somewhere today.'

'He'll behave,' Annabella promised, tapping Mac's forearm with one scarlet tipped nail whilst thinking a metre long, twenty centimetre wide, strip of material into existence. 'Or I'll gag him.'

Less than a minute into his explanation, Buster was again interrupted. This time by the appearance of a tray filled with steaming mugs, a large Clementine cake, serviettes and several bread-and-butter plates.

'I'm getting a wee bit tired of this,' Mac barked. 'Iffen ye

59

is, or is ta be, our Master. I'd have ta say ye ways of communicating 'tis bloody ill-mannered. And ye can come out, for I'll nay bite ye.'

Ripping the end off a large A4-sized envelope, previously slotted between two of the china mugs, Mac pulled out a piece of ragged paper and without bothering to read it, handed the unfolded the note to Jank.

'Coffee anyone?'

Still trying to contain the giggles Mac's gruff remarks had raised Michaela blurted, 'Jank honey, forget the flopping drinks and just tell us what the damn thing said.'

She wasn't sure as to what their Master was up to, since it was fairly obvious his invisible self was within listening distance, but it didn't stop Jannelle from uttering her own less than kind taunt.

'As much as I hate to admit it, the big Scot's quite right,' she snickered. 'It is bloody rude especially considering how much emphasis the man puts on etiquette. Nevertheless, he is our Master, and if you ever do get to meet him it'll pay to remember he oft behaves like an overgrown kid.'

Jank had known for several decades the lineage of the person his parents, Jannelle and Buster, primarily worked for and had frequently heard his mother grumble in a similar way about the man's quirky sense of humour. So, when she queried the contents of the missive for the second time, he picked up one of the mugs and mock scolded, 'I just did. Weren't you paying attention? It politely asks if anyone wants a coffee.'

'Thanks sweetie.' Ignoring the exasperation which leapt through Michaela's apology and ran amok over Mac's long face. Annabella took a sip from the china beaker Jank had given her before turning to add a curious, 'What I would like to know is what I'm to do here. How do the rest of us decide on who does what, Buster? Is there a precedent set anywhere?'

'By the charters the latter plains adhere to, it's usually decided by a person's community service, work or self-interest qualifications and if Mistress Fate is feeling kindly disposed towards you, your personal preference. But as we've yet to decide whether or not to follow their models I suppose it's up to us,' Buster shrugged.

Her large blue eyes twinkled with a facetious glimmer when Jannelle suggested, 'You could always flip a coin.'

'In other words, leave it up ta tha' Gods.'

'One God mate,' William sharply corrected. 'He might be called by many names by many cultures, nonetheless there's only ever been one First to Be and Creator of All.'

''Tis nowt but a figure of speech laddie thus no disrespect was intended nor 'tis there any reason to get uppity.'

Though Kat smiled at Mac's friendly reprimand she slumped back into her chair, the enormity of it all crashing over her as she tilted back her head.

Momentarily distracted by the audaciously decorated ceiling. The petite blonde's heart began to thump erratically when a softly welcoming, *Nice isn't it,* flowed into her mind.

The most important cube of the young woman's remaining memories exploding in a hailstorm of information as she tentatively murmured, 'Bro?'

'Sorry missed that,' Jank said. 'What did you say?'

A vague resonance of music and tender, *Shush please,* urging Kat to by-pass Jank's question to say, 'Can you hear that?'

Like Kat, the first strains of music her companion's heard were barely audible. But as the tempo hastened and the volume grew. The strumming of piano keys, haunting wail of bagpipes and growl of didgeridoo's rose to a deafening crescendo. Only to be cut off mid-beat by the four downward spiralling envelopes that had dived off the highest of chamber's wooden beams.

The movement of his massive leg jiggling up and down in excitement made the carpeted floor vibrate around them as an eager Buster declared, 'Bet ya a dozen witchetty grubs we'll have some answers in a minute.'

'Yuck, thanks but no thanks,' Jank shuddered.

Combing through the pile of missives which had circled the table several times before settling themselves beside his drink, the good-looking young man promptly delivered each to its intended owner with a practiced flick of his wrist.

'Mine says I'm to be Chief of Security,' Kat said in disbelief.

'Mac?' William prompted.

Quickly scanning the small sheet of parchment Mac flapped under his nose, it was Jank who replied, 'He's our Training Master and I'm to be the Master Technician.'

Easily collating the responsibilities of the eight positions normally used to govern the Afterlife's numerous plains. Buster acknowledged the importance of what would become their plain's final managing role with a half-risen bow and a touch of his former arrogance.

'Therefore, Annabella's our Chief Administrator.'

The doubt Michaela saw darken Annabella's eyes to a deep jade brought a brief smile of understanding to her face. And since the other three all wore similar miens, she offered some gentle encouragement to the rather flummoxed quartet.

'Big tasks people,' she said. 'However, you may recall or

will come to remember, well excluding Mac, of course… Either Bust, Jan, Will, or myself have at one time or another held similar roles. So one would think we're also meant to be your Mentors. Bust, as you're the Master Archivist would you mind running through a short Induction with Mac?'

'Not at all dear lady… Unfortunately, we're beginning the settlement of a new plain and therefore have to critique an Induction before implementing it. Thus, because that particular job comes under the purview of the Training Collator it may take a while,' Buster laughed.

'Oooh yeah, sorry. Didn't quite think that one through, did I?'

'It's a lot to process, babe,' William said as he stood up. 'Perhaps now's a good time for a break. Who's up to exploring this new home of ours?'

'How?' Annabella queried.

'Same way as we got here one would imagine,' William said.

As she lifted the fluffy kitten off her lap Michaela thought an assortment of toys, a rug and a bowl of water, plus one filled with a variety of the feline's favourite nibbles into the nearest corner of the room.

'Bro's about somewhere, so you stay here, Miss. You knew if you took on the persona of a kitten, not the ageless feline you've come to be, you'd be treated like one until your body grows up again. We'll most likely be back for dinner.'

Unable to hear what else was being said over Sophia's deafeningly meowed complaints. Michaela hurriedly lowered her to the floor and once upright, wondered why Jannelle still remained seated when their companions were either standing or like she now was, in the process of rising.

63

The Chief Justice's grim demeanour and dully spoken, '...
And we've enough bloody work to keep us busy for the next
ten decades.'

An unwelcome response to her private musing.

Bent over again like a half-opened pocketknife, Buster
stared at his exotic looking friend and mumbled an unhappy,
'Buut...'

'Buut,' Jannelle mocked, keeping her countenance
blander than unseasoned damper as she added a longer, more
protracted, 'Buuuuut?'

'I... Oh nothing,' Buster spluttered, wishing he knew why
she was being such a killjoy when he, himself, found the itch
to explore almost uncontrollable.

'I... Oh nothing... Well, well, weeell...' No longer able
to control the mischievous smile trembling at the corners of
her mouth Jannelle added a jubilant, 'We do need to know
what we've got to deal with, don't we?'

By the time the Nano second it took him to realise she'd
once again been pushing his buttons flew away. Buster's hands
had already spun the woman's chair around till the top of her
head came level with the taut muscles bunched halfway up his
thighs.

Powerless against his enormous bulk, Jannelle found
herself hauled up and over the Master Archivist's shoulder like
she weighed no more than an empty spud bag.

'I'm off,' Buster whooped, paying no heed to the fists she
pummelled against his back as he pumped the air with his free
hand. 'Who's coming with me?'

'Och laddie, put the wee lass down for we all are. Dinna
ye ken, we're supposed ta be forming a clan,' Mac said, his
disapproving words melding with Annabella's, 'Oh put her

down, you big oaf,' and William's, 'Behave mate.'

Scarlet faced, but with her feet now firmly replanted on the floor, a giggling Jannelle said she was well used to Buster's caveman like antics. Nevertheless, used to them or not, as they'd circled up a means of retaliation found a home in her lively brain.

'Bustie revenge is a dish best served cold…' she vowed. 'Thus, you're on notice my friend.'

His plaintive, 'You started it,' filed away for future debates as all thought, *Outside.*

OFF PLAIN: GOD'S TOOTH WOMAN
WHERE'VE YE LANDED US

With stomach roiling and nausea once again rising in her throat, Michaela released the hands she held. Gulping a few gasps of air in the vain hope it would help, her eyes flashed open when Mac cursed, 'God's tooth woman where've ye landed us 'tis like a slaughterhouse in there.'

Flinching when a round of explosions shook the ground, Jank replied with thinly veiled sarcasm, 'What? The sound of mortar fire doesn't give you an inkling?'

'And whilst I'm not exactly sure why I'm to blame, fair bung in the middle of someone's bloody war is my guess Mac,' Michaela moaned in disgust. 'Everyone okay?'

'Yeah, just dandy Mick,' Kat muttered. 'Get us out of here before we all get killed.'

Curling one side of his mouth up in response to Kat's dark jest, Jank peered over the wooden half-wall they'd materialised behind.

Both humour and colour drained from his face as he turned back to his companions to say, 'It's a hospital of sorts and aren't we supposed to be the only souls on our plain?'

'That's what was indicated. However, it's been known for several continents to be colonised simultaneously. Still...' Pausing to push back his slouch hat and scratch at his forehead Buster added, 'Still, I think we must've triggered a side trip.'

Jannelle's brief, 'Well, don't ask me.'

66

Lost when the door behind them crashed open and two men came barrelling in, blood leaching from the rough field dressings wrapped around the stomach of the man they carried between them.

'Here, take him,' the shorter of two soldiers snapped, directing his court order towards Annabella who happened to be closest to the door.

Left with no alternative when the man's arm was flung over her shoulders. Annabella's knees angled out as the total weight of the unconscious man hit her slender frame. Thankfully, with one swift forward step later, William was there to help her lower the wounded man to the straw strewn floor.

After rapidly scanning all of the eight's uniforms the corporal offered up a reluctant salute to Buster then added a brusque, 'Lieutenant, if you're planning on living for much longer you need to get Captain Smith and everyone else the hell out of here.'

At Buster's silent nod of compliance, the man sketched another rough salute. The noise of the outside world only slightly diminishing when the door banged shut behind the two departing soldiers.

As Kat sunk to the floor her appalled, 'Let me look at him,' ran together with Michaela's, 'I'll go and find this Captain Smith.'

But it was Jannelle's sharply hissed, 'No, not yet,' which stalled any further comments and ended in a calmer. 'Think for a moment, guys. Buster, any idea where or when we might be?'

'Now that I've had a minute to study our clothes, weapons and the uniforms those chaps were wearing I reckon it's the Great War. Thus, somewhere between 1914 and 1918.'

'Nice aren't they,' Annabella looked up to grimace, eying the long skirts, blood-stained aprons and blue blouses she and the other three women wore before returning her gaze to the tattered khaki uniforms of her male companions.

'When did we change?' Mac grunted, disregarding the heavy rifle slung over his shoulder to fiddle with the holster of the handgun strapped to his belt. 'For we dinna leave with these wee things.'

'It varies and jeez be careful with that mate. It's probably loaded.'

'Och laddie, won't be much good if it isn't,' Mac scoffed. 'I've read a bit about these and have a wee bit of experience with guns iffen that's what's concerning you... Mind, 'tis the first time I've seen held such a tasty weapon... How many er, bullets I think they're called, does it have?'

'Eight and don't point the bloody thing at me,' Buster winced as he shoved the gun Mac was brandishing about to one side. 'And if you have to use it remember to count your shots... Many a soul went up yonder because they either couldn't count or forgot to keep track.'

'Well, we certainly aren't there now. His souls just left,' Kat quietly announced as she closed the soldier's lifeless eyes and straightened a wayward strand of his matted hair.

'First time?'

Angrily dashing away the tears trickling down her pale cheeks, the petite girl tenderly placed the dead soldier's head on a pillow of straw. Then slowly got to her feet before replying to William's oral question, and the unspoken one she saw in his eyes, with a stark, 'No, I've witnessed plenty of deaths, so yes, I'm sure.'

'In that case this has to be an active call out,' William

sighed. 'Mac, looks like your Induction into plain life went down the gurgler.'

'Dinna fret ye self about that,' Mac yelped when another round of explosions vibrated up through the sturdy soles of their footwear. 'Ye can fill me in later.'

Clutching at Mac's sleeve to steady her trembling body so she could also stand Annabella cried, 'Time to move people. That one felt awfully close.'

'Not really that close, but you're right,' Buster said.

'Whist iffen we're dead that won't concern us, will it?'

'It does those poor buggers, sunshine. Which I surmise is the whole point of us being here,' Buster growled, and with one hand held up for silence, the other pointing to the insignia on his collar he declared in a tone which left no room for argument, 'I'm the ranking officer, so I'll go find this Captain Smith. Jan you're with me… The rest of you stay here.'

The bright sunlight shining through the bullet pocked roof gave the otherwise unlit room Buster and Jannelle entered a surreal appearance. Piles of used and unused medical equipment were tidily stacked against the majority of the three outer walls, yet the earthen floor was barely visible, eaten up by rows of stretcher prone men.

A fleeting smile lightened a thin woman's haggard face as she glanced up from the papers spread out on the table in front of her and saw the approaching couple.

Lifting a weary hand, she straightened her wimple before saluting. Her tentative smile vanishing as Buster crisply answered in kind then relayed the disturbing information they'd been asked to pass on.

For a moment the Captain stood as still as a poker while staring up into Buster's long brown eyes. She'd learnt of the

Australian Aborigines in school but nothing she'd read had ever indicated they'd be promoted past the lowest of defence ratings.

'We've too many seriously injured men to be able to do that, sir,' she slowly countered. 'The ambulances won't be back for at least an hour and a half, and there are only three of us here.'

'Plus, six more of us,' Buster gently revealed. 'Which will have to do.'

Despite the fact he out ranked her, and was by far the largest man she'd ever seen, it was their desperate plight more than the concerned honesty she read on his ebony face which convinced her to trust him.

As Buster saw the wary hope scramble into in the Captain's red rimmed eyes and a decisive nod of acceptance elevate her chin. He turned his head to bellow across the room, 'Jank, Mac, take a look outside and see if there's any type of transport we can use. Everyone else start packing.'

'You heard the Lieutenant, get up ya lazy bastards,' the officer lying on the stretcher beside Jannelle roared. 'If you can move, move. Take what you can. Don't leave anything of value for the bloody Huns,' and with a far crisper salute than the first Buster had received, extended his bandaged hands.

'God bless you, sir.'

'You sure about this, Bust?' Jannelle whispered, tugging on the immense man's sleeve as soon as he'd released the war aged officer's hands. 'Bust?'

And even though she'd quite often experienced Buster's suddenly stilled posture and blank look, Jannelle jabbed the point of her elbow into his body and murmured his name again.

Shaking his head as he stopped Jannelle's angled arm from connecting with the base of his hip a second time, Buster leant over to say against her ear, 'Save your energy ya big bully. 'Cause I've been told we're to get them to the main hospital.'

OFF PLAIN: TRANSPORT?

Crouched behind a water barrel, the only cover along the side wall the buildings door had opened out off, Mac and Jank did a quick visual scout of the area.

Barren hills ran down onto a broad paddock and due to the bright, midmorning sunshine the battlefield before them was displayed in all its grim reality. There had been a brief period of quiet before they'd come out. But now the whine of bullets and the boom of artillery shells streaming back and forth between the two opposing armies drowned out anything but the closest of sounds.

'Give me a few minutes,' Jank shouted. 'I'll check none of the bastards have outflanked us.'

'Aye, good thinking and ye should announce ye self or I may shoot ye by mistake.'

Grabbing the man by his arm Jank snarled, 'Get with the programme mate... Our bodies die the same way anyone else's in this period of history would so just make sure you bloody well don't.'

'Laddie 'twas nought but a smidge of black humour, ye are in no danger from me... Stop ye blathering and be gone with ye.'

It had taken Jank longer than he'd expected to circle back to far end side of the building and not fully convinced Mac wouldn't shoot first, ask later, he yelled out a brief all clear.

Nevertheless, he waited till he heard the man's gruff response before rounding the last corner leading back to the water barrel.

Shivering in disbelief at the wide spread devastation, Mac's bleak eyes flickered between the direction of Jank's voice and the destructive work of the men below as he nodded towards the sturdy building across from where they stood, then pointed to the closest of the naked hills.

'The barn it is and once again I find me self in brutal times laddie,' he morosely muttered when Jank glumly waved away his question of transport. 'Aye and 'tis a good thing we weren't any later getting here or else it mayhap have been a wee bit uncomfortable for the lasses and lads inside. I dinna think those chappies on yon hill are wearing the same outfit as ye and I.'

Looking down the long barrel and through the site of his rifle, Jank groaned. The spiked helmets of the soldiers swarming down over the foothill clearly defining who was who, and unless help arrived, which side would soon have the upper hand.

'Shite no,' he cursed. 'Go, I've got your back.'

Somewhat relieved his rapid search of the barn's interior had come up empty of human inhabitants, Mac walked to the doorway. Signalling the all-clear, he watched Jank skirt the worst of the war-torn ground. Its sorry state evidence this area had been at the forefront of more than one theatre of the current war's angry dispute. Yet when Jank's eyes had adjusted to the dim light inside the barn, he could only view the wagon Mac now slouched against with disbelief.

'Flaming oath mate. What are you planning on doing with that? Haul it by hand? Dammit to hell this is a bloody waste of time,' he swore. 'And what the blue blazes have you got in there?'

Cautiously moving his hand towards his wriggling pocket. Mac laughed as a silky black head and two tiny paws popped out between its woollen flaps.

'Will ye look at that… Miss Sophie was allowed ta come with us after ta all.' Warning her to stay put, Mac intensified his next words with a firmer, 'Missy stop that or I'll smack ye,' when Sophia swiped at him with her sharp claws.

Unable to detach both her paws from the rough material of his coat at the same time. Mac uttered a string of profanity when the kitten's razor-sharp teeth sunk into the soft, unprotected pad of one thumb while her nails imbedded themselves into the palm of his other hand.

Repeating his colourful language as he yanked his hands away from the volatile bundle of fur. Mac surprised Jank when he froze at the sight of the blood welling out from his punctured skin.

Unperturbed by the damage she'd inflicted, the kitten made the most of their momentary lack of attention. Retracting her claws with unseemly haste, she freed herself from the confines of the pocket then jumped to the floor and hissed her displeasure.

'Put the little pest back where she came from,' Jank ordered, quite happily snubbing the looks of ruffled indignation Sophia attached to her noisy outcry. 'We need to keep moving.'

'Ye did try ta thinking something up didn't ye?'

'It doesn't work here…'

'Perhaps, we can only use what's available in this era laddie. Did ye think of that?'

'As I'm not up to date with every bloody period of history that's not much help is it.'

''Tis the Great War of 1914 the big man told us, dinna he not?' Mac puffed whilst chasing the elusive kitten from one side of the barn to the other. 'Come on laddie use ye brain.'

Walking over to take a closer look at the old, yet sturdy enough looking wagon. The annoyance Jank felt at Mac's comments rattled through his rapid, 'What the blazes do you think I've been doing? Like I told you, thinking as we mean it doesn't work here. I can't produce a bloody band-aid let alone truck or ambulance.'

Unfussed by Jank's displeasure and aware the minutes were speeding by, Mac gave up on the kitten to concentrate so hard his face went bright red.

'Sorry, thought I'd try again but nowt.'

'Perhaps, it's not as heavy as it looks,' Jank grunted, accepting Mac's short apology with a curt nod while they each took hold of the oaken shaft of the wagon and pulled on it with all their strength.

'This won't do laddie. Loaded we'll nay be able to move it iffen we have twenty men ta pull it.'

Any alternatives appear to be as elusive as our new plain, Jank was thinking when Mac let go of the shaft and went to bend under his suddenly up stretched arms.

Jank's peripheral vision had seen what Mac had, but his feelings of helplessness caused the arm he used to hold the man back with to connect harder than it probably should've done.

'Uh ah, this time it's me going,' he said, ignoring the man's oomph of escaping air. 'The little brats got one more chance or risks becoming cannon fodder.'

Moving almost faster than the puss, Jank peered around the door Sophia had just slipped through. And felt his heart change tempo when the warm breath of something much larger than himself feathered his cheek.

Tightly squeezing his eyes together, Mac mumbled a swift prayer then yelped in amazement, 'Laddie 'tis me ears playing the joker or 'twas that what I thought it 'twas.'

'Yep, and jeez he's a big one.'

'Miss Puss? And 'tis there a harness…'

'No to the former but as to the rest… Check it out yourself old man.'

Amazed by the sensory input his ears and eyes were jabbing him with, Mac's hand shook as he reached out to touch the huge stallion's satin smooth coat. Studying this, then that part of the harness he whispered, 'Lord, 'tis more of ye magic youngster.'

'Nah, nothing of the sort,' Jank scoffed. 'It's just coincidental.'

'Well, I'll nay argue, but if that's the case mind ye head. 'Tis about ta snow pink cows.'

'Kat,' Jannelle said as she propped the last bag of supplies against the wall. 'Could you take a quick gander outside to see if there's any sign of the boys.'

With a brief nod of compliance Kat smiled down at the soldier lying on the stretcher at her feet. The last to arrive at the makeshift hospital. His bandaged chest hid the worst of his injuries one of the nurses had murmured when she'd seen Kat's face blanch at the sight of the young sergeant's broken body.

Both of his legs ended with bandaged stumps. The right

above the knee, the left at the ankle. Even so, it was the involuntarily clenching and unclenching of his hands that saw a further band of distress tighten around the young girl's heart.

Told the last of the makeshift hospital's anaesthetics had run out before the sun had completed a quarter of its day's travel, Kat knew he had to be in agony. But it hadn't dimmed the friendliness of his smile nor stop him introducing himself with a chatty, 'Me Mum named me Ertlly but the lads call me Helper. Dance with me when we get home?'

So impulsively leaning over to kiss the young man's cheek, Kat took the handgun he held out to her. Assuring him she knew how to use it, she stepped sideways to slowly open the door.

Scanning the yard for the third time, her eyes had returned to the stone structure opposite when several large digits wrapped themselves around its doorframe. The hairs on the back of her neck rising as she cocked the weapon and watched the barn door open. Then expelled her last intake of breath in a soundless whistle when she recognised the fiery red hair flowing out from under Mac's battered slouch hat.

'Lassie, get them out here,' Mac yelled when he caught sight of her small face. 'We've a horse and cart.'

'No vehicles?'

'Nay and 'tis men only. Ye canna worry about anything else.'

Hoping to find that the kitten had sneaked back into the barn. Mac turned to scour its bare rafters again before ending his fruitless search by kicking a half open bundle of hay so hard most of it bounced of the far wall.

His repeated calling of her name remained unanswered

while he backtracked his earlier steps out the door and along the side wall, only to scream in concerned frustration when neither sight nor sound disclosed the puss's whereabouts.

'Mac, hurry up, we're ready to go.'

The fretful worry in Annabella's voice saw the reluctant Scot hurry back to the wagon. The latest flurry of shelling rocking the ground around them as he took the reins from Jank. A resigned sigh preceding the click of his tongue which urged the stallion forward while he prayed that wherever Sophia was, the tiny feline would come to no harm.

The weight of the wounded taxed the stallion to the limits of his strength but with mud coursing up his flanks with every step of his massive hooves, Mac steered him straight through rain filled puddles. Avoiding only the largest of the bomb generated craters pockmarking the rough track in their race for the relative safety of the allied camp.

Half an hour later the Scotsman guided the horse as far off the muddy road the forest of trees edging its eastern side would allow. Abdicating the road, such as it was, for the convoy of canvas topped trucks and jeeps that were almost upon them.

Whistles for the woman and an occasional, 'She'll be right cobber we'll get 'em for you,' leaving no doubt as to the nationality of the foot soldiers jogging behind the vehicles.

'Aussie, Aussie, Aussie,' Jank chanted, his cheer a loud salutation for the sacrifice the earnest young men who milled round, then past them, were prepared to expend.

Hampered more by the clumps of sticky earth caked to her boots, and the voluminous hem of her frock sodden from where it dragged in the clayish soil, than the heavy rifle and backpack she'd propped against the wheel of the wagon.

Kat's, 'Oy, oy, oy,' was followed by a grunted curse when the stick she'd been scrapping the sole of her boot with went spinning from her hand.

Picking up the piece that had landed at his feet. Buster lobbed it back with a warning to watch what they said as that particular phrase wouldn't be coined for at least another fifty years or so. Their combined apology failing to compete with the stuttering clamour of a distressed aeroplane.

Identifying the stricken fighter plane diving towards them by the distinct blue, white and red target that Buster knew would be painted both above, and beneath its wings he shouted, 'Sop Worth Camel, she's one of ours.'

And while he fervently wished for a different outcome the immense man couldn't help but think it would be a certain death for both plane and pilot when the ailing craft dropped from sight beneath the treeline.

Yet after a short, eerie void of soundlessness came the screech of shredded metal and splintering of timber as the aeroplane battered a path through the plantation of pine trees.

Unable to judge if, or where, it would escape the forests clinging arms, William and those around him hurled themselves across the wagon. Their bodies forming a human shield over the wounded men only moments before the crumpled aircraft burst from the woodland, less than a wingspan from where they lay.

Just visible through the noxious plumes of black smoke and searing heat of the flames pouring from its engine. The pilot's face showed a mixture of terror and fierce determination as he fought to control the dying aircraft.

But it was a fight he wouldn't win. The 'Camel' slamming into the chopped-up field opposite the wagon with such jarring force, the earth once again shook, and the plane's wheel struts snapped.

Bouncing once, twice, then thrice more before fusing to the ground. The burning craft slid along the paddock felling the few trees standing in its way as if they were mere matchsticks. Its final resting place, the charred remains of a German tank.

With fisted arm raised in defiant victory the pilot leapt from the fiery pyre, relishing his reprieve from death while embracing the euphoria of beating the odds of war once more. The last column of infantry running to surround the whooping man as Mac shooed those capable of walking from the wagon.

Following in the jumbled ruts of previous traffic, it was another fifteen minutes of hard travelling until the laden wagon began to breach the crest of a steep incline. The last Captain Smith told them, before they'd reach the relative safety of the Allied camp.

The Captain had had little to do with her country's partners prior to the short week she'd been with the Allied Offensive. And there'd been nothing in her strict English upbringing, medical training or short time at the as an Army Corps Captain, to prepare her for the quirky camaraderie which flowed with such ease between the different ranks of the Australians.

Nor had she have ever anticipated riding through the French countryside; supporting a gun-shot patient whilst sitting on the front bench seat of a horse drawn cart, unashamedly listening to the outlandish banter that flowed back and forth between the eight strangers. The Scotsman who now walked alongside the horse's huge head, its primary instigator.

Halted for a short respite where the hill momentarily flattened out. Mac dropped his water filled hat on the ground beneath the Clydesdale's sweat lathered nose then began to survey what could be seen of the downward track, and the field blanketed with tight rows of tents that was only just visible over the treetops.

'Methinks so long as the brakes continue ta work the downward trip twill be easier. By the looks of things the worst 'tis behind us.'

'Looks like a 'M.A.S.H.' set. Pity we couldn't think up some modern stuff to help 'em out,' William said as he tipped the last half of his canteen into Mac's damp hat.

'We learnt a lot thanks to your infatuation with that series,' Jank said with a small grin.

'Yeah, we did.' Leaving the man she'd been helping chatting with his mates, Michaela walked the few extra steps needed to wrap an arm around her soulmate's waist. 'And if you're talking wish lists, a float chair or two wouldn't go astray either. Midgets and feet deep mud don't go together.'

'Mud's bloody mud Mick, size doesn't enter into it,' Jannelle disagreed, proving her own point when the next step she took saw her stumble over a hidden tree root. Grasping a fistful of air instead of the hoped-for material belonging to the smaller woman's skirts. She barely managed to avoid landing face down in the middle of a muddy puddle.

Quick to lean over to help her up. Michaela and Annabella struggled to stifle their giggles as irate woman spluttered, 'I've bloody well… Had a bloody enough of this, it bloody stinks.'

Sweat and the odd splatter of mud only added to the exotic beauty of Jannelle's face. Still the noisy, involuntarily sounds

81

coming from her throat ensured everyone within hearing range knew of the woman's on-going discontentment.

'Tisk, tisk, are ye right? 'Tis a mouthful of dirty words ye've been a spouting woman,' a grinning Mac dared to complain. 'Ye ken mud is good for ye complexion, dinna ye?'

Jannelle's sharp, 'Belt the hell up, you fool,' ending with another spurt of harsher cussing.

OFF PLAIN: HOME?

Although the downward journey wasn't scare free, the first mud slide almost taking three of the party with it, the second the rear end of the wagon. The final thirty minutes had been the hardest.

Greeted by a quagmire where the base of the hill met unfenced paddocks, the road disappeared. The half mile of swamp until it re-appeared again, left unattended by the momentum of the current engagement.

By skirting the worst of its water hidden dangers, a further mile and the cost of a badly broken arm had been added to their journey. So it wasn't surprising a ragged cheer went up when Mac lined the back of the wagon up with the doorway of a pair of co-joined marques.

Three times longer in length than they were in width. The bright red crosses painted on their steeped roofs was a welcome indication that the canvas draped poles covered the bustling activity of the camp's hospital.

Grumbling to himself as he ran his eyes over the stallion's steaming, mud dulled coat, whose drooping head and heaving body was an unspoken plea to at least have the drying muck removed from his long mane. Mac's wished for bucket of hot, soapy water remained an unrequited thought as his fingers began to comb through the matted hair. Moving around to deal with the huge animals' other side, his attention roved from the willingly undertaken invitation to the medical staff who swarmed around them. The attending doctor's calm orders quickly emptying the cart of all but the splatters of darkening blood that stained its wooden floor.

When the tempo of the past ten minutes finally dribbled away to nothing, Buster found himself standing between Captain Smith and the two nurses who'd also been on shift at the triage hospice.

'Well ladies,' he said. 'I'm afraid it's time we went.'

Told to grab a quick cup of tea but to forget about the dubious comfort of their army cots for several more hours, the gallant young women's smiles of farewell were tainted with weariness.

As was Captain Smith's parting, 'Thank you again, safe travels. Without your aid we might all have died, so this act of kindness will never be forgotten. You will be in my prayers until the end of this wretched business and beyond.'

A coil of heavy silence lay over them after the nurses walked away. William was the first to stir, dropping a kiss on top of Michaela's head with a murmured, 'Home, babe?'

Only just catching Michaela's soft response. Mac jerked his thumb towards the men sitting around a water trough several feet from where they stood and bluntly stated he needed to give the stallion another drink before they went anywhere.

Nor did anyone else speak again whilst the Scotsman was gone. Taking the returning clip clop of the Clydesdale's hooves to interrupt her glum thoughts enough for Michaela to say, 'Shall we see if we can think our way out of here?'

'Mickey... Um, everybody, perhaps we're meant to stay and help? There's a whole war happening here and with the exception of Mac it affected us all.'

'No. If we can go, we go,' Buster sharply countermanded, then surprising himself more than anyone else, pulled the ashen faced Annabella into his arms. 'Sorry, but we know the right side wins, and our other chores might well be considered more important.'

'True,' the svelte woman reluctantly conceded as she snuggled into the warm comfort of his stomach. 'But I'd suggest going elsewhere before trying.'

'Mmm yes, for we're not exactly alone, are we?' William's subdued undertone was similar to Annabella's had been as he too cocked a thumb towards the soldiers sitting around the water barrel. 'Even considering the horrors they've undoubtedly survived, it would probably scare the bejeezers out of them if we were here one second and gone the next.'

While the eight companions looked around for some measure of privacy the beckoning summons of distant canons was superseded by the thunderous revving of engines.

Dotting the ground with waves of shadows the squadron of departing aircraft's answering song, a defiant challenge to the Grim Reaper as they flew to their countrymen's defence. The muted chorus left in its wake mourning the loss of so many lives in a war finally ignited by the murderous assassination of one man's nephew.

'Perhaps behind the hospital.' Already moving as she spoke, the Chief Justice bobbed between the guy ropes which kept the nearest marquee and the row of tents beside it, upright. Rapidly scrutinising the vacant area they backed onto, she called over her shoulder, 'This'll do.'

Willing to bet her next ten cappuccino's that Mac wouldn't agree, Michaela licked her lips as she stared up into the red head's fatigued face.

'Er Mac… Perhaps you might find a spot to tether the horse?'

'Nay… Nay lass, such a bonnie brave boy should come with us.'

'And if he doesn't make it back, then what?' William said, stepping around Michaela to pat the enormous animal.

'Well, he'll go ta the holding lanes where the souls first gather,' Mac frowned. 'Ye've all been there and say its nay that bad, then mayhap he'll come ta us.'

'You said he's a brave one. So dying before his time seems a tad mean just to keep him with you,' William starkly rebuked.

'Oh… Oh aye man, I dinna think of it that way,' Mac almost sobbed, a slow fifteen seconds dragging by while he dabbed at the flecks of dirt freckling the bright red poppies etched into the stallion's harness. The result of the expressions that skimmed across his eyes explained with an emotionless, 'I'll bring him around the back though. Twill be a bit quieter for him there.'

With that said, the troubled man stepped in the path of a passing orderly.

'Ken ye help me laddie?' He hurriedly asked. 'I canna take me horse where I'm a going, orders ye understand. He's had a drink so iffen I leave him behind yon big abode can ye mayhap get someone to clean him up and give him something ta eat for me?'

'Too right I will sir. Be there as soon as I've delivered this.' Tucking a ragged folder under his arm, a wide grin spread across the tall youth's face as he reached up to gently rubbed the stallion's nose. 'I've got a few of these beauties back in Tassie. He'll be in good hands with me, that's a promise.'

It took Mac nearly five minutes to find a laneway wide enough for the huge Clydesdale and wagon to navigate then several more until they wound their way back to where his companions waited for them, circled up and ready to go.

Tying the reins to a wooden post before giving the horse a last parting caress, a stray gust of wind wrapped the hem of Mac's greatcoat around the stallion's fetlocks.

But the quietly whimpering man didn't notice, and wouldn't have spared it much thought if he had, for he was too busy grasping Kat and Annabella's hands.

The warmth of their fingers a sought for comfort as he pleaded, *Keep Miss Sophie and the big boy safe. And aye, home please Lord.*

ON PLAIN: HOME?

One by one, the eight found themselves falling from the sky towards a large Billabong. Its tannin-stained water surrounded on all sides by a wide swathe of white sand and a circle of flowering gumtrees carpeted with dense undergrowth.

Lovely though it was, the rapidly shrinking view was spared only the scantest of attention. The remainder solely focused on minimising the impact of their speeding descent.

'Thank goodness thinking works again,' Jank shouted at the back of Kat's head, finding his body refreshed and mind going into overdrive as he followed her down a bright red slippery slide. His long legs easily avoiding the dark brown water rippling around its feet.

'Yes, therefore I'm checking the area and you're coming with me.'

Signing to Buster that they were going to do a quick reconnaissance, who responded with a casual thumbs up from the comfort of his leather lounge chair which floated fifty centimetres off the ground, and several metres away from the water, the pair broke into an easy jog.

'I think we managed our re-entry better than some, don't you?' Kat laughed as she stopped where the sloping sand ran into the tree line and glanced backwards.

'Bloody site drier anyway... Me thinks Mum needs some more practise, 'cause she'd only get five out of ten for her landing.'

The woman at the centre of the pair's amusement had squealed in dismay when she found herself upside down some ten metres above the large stretch of water.

With wildly flailing arms and legs, Michaela dropped towards the ground. The Ambassadress's fertile imagination the only reason her posterior met the centre of a large trampoline instead of her head. Regrettably, two bounces and one-half somersault later, it connected with the sandy base of the shallow pond.

Having missed the padded edge of the trampoline by a meagre millimetre Jannelle clung to a large, red exercise ball. Already saturated from her own somewhat inelegant landing in the brackish water she was in no mood for what came next.

Because although Michaela weighed under fifty kilograms, her clumsy arrival triggered a shower of water which managed to drench whatever part of the Chief Justice's body that had, until then, remained dry.

Knuckling the water from her eyes while she swivelled her head, Jannelle glared across at Buster and the three souls that sat with him. The sound of their laughter making her normally unblemished skin mottle with dots of embarrassed anger.

On you, she thought, a smirk of satisfaction disintegrating her ire when they became the victims of her numerous, and extremely well aimed, spouts of liquid.

Not to be out done nor overly pleased with her own less than graceful reappearance. Michaela made sure the ones she swiftly replicated also found their intended targets.

'Och ye wee brats there's no reason for that, for we dinna put ye there.'

'Oops sorry, accident,' Jannelle giggled. 'Need a towel,

Mac?'

'Nay woman… But ye do,' Mac growled.

And as more of the brackish water flew between the six. Screams of laughter threaded with an occasional mild curse continued to ring out until Buster eventually called a halt to their antics.

'So, we made it back,' William rhetorically stated.

'Aye maybe, least ways the airs pure and our wee thoughts work again,' Mac said as he looked around to add a concerned, 'Where are the wee lad and lassie? For their nowt here and what now? 'Tis no buildings here. Thus, its nay the place we left from.'

'Well, they were here before… Oh here they come now so we might have some more info in a moment,' Annabella answered, her extended arm waving to where Jank and Kat strolled along the wide beach with the reins of a huge, familiar horse loosely wrapped around the lad's hand.

Michaela might've been glad to see them, but it was mainly anger that stomped through her voice when she yelled out, 'What the hell were you two thinking of? You shouldn't have gone off like that.'

Refusing to elevate her voice. Kat waited until the pair's quickening steps drew them close enough to be easily heard then calmly replied, 'Michaela you're wrong… As Chief of Security, it was exactly what I needed to do and since I didn't know our precise location, I thought it prudent to take Jank with me. Especially seeing you lot were so busy mucking about.'

'You vanished before you could have seen any of our behaviour,' William contested.

Stone faced, Kat tapped the watch like armlet on her wrist,

which most of them hadn't even realised they were now all wearing, before firing fact after fact up at her frowning uncle.

'Actually, we didn't. Nevertheless, that can wait for a second. Safely coded with each soul's DNA. We now have cameras mounted with heat seeking, automatic weapons strategically placed in every fifth tree which faces this body of water and an outer ring of the same ilk aimed towards the foothills.

'Add a trio of armed, aerial spy cams; elevation one, three and five hundred metres, range ten kilometres… I'd say we're relatively secure irrespective of whichever plain we happen to be on.'

In a tone as crisp as his petite cousin's had been Jank rounded out Kat's information with a caustic, 'Besides, Bust knew what we were doing, and our Chief of Security put the first in place before I bet you lot even blinked. Finalising the latter whilst watching mum's rather inept touchdown.'

'I was about to mention that,' Buster nodded.

'Jeez Bust you…' However, seeing she'd merely thought the pair were yet to arrive back, which was quite a frequent occurrence with group missions, Michaela swapped both ambiance and hastily chewed up words for a much smoother, 'I stand corrected. Sorry I yelled.'

'Ditto,' William wryly drawled. 'The horse?'

'We found him on the other side of the Billabong and knew softy here would be pleased to see him,' Jank replied, handing the reins to a delighted Mac as he accepted their apologies with an off-hand nod.

'Aye that I am laddie, that I am,' Mac confirmed, wiping an emotional tear away.

Keener to impart what they had seen than to discuss the

mystery of the stallion Kat knelt down and drew a map in the damp sand.

'What we've seen is a smallish Billabong encased by about a three-hundred-meter span of sand, trees and thick underbrush,' she explained, pointing to each in turn. 'Which appears to be the central point of another ten kilometres of lush grazing land that butts up against what we're pretty positive are the same foothills and mountains you guys were banging on about this morning. Yet we didn't see any other animals apart from the horse.'

'Plus, mosquitoes,' Jank threw in, his swiftly up raised hand shooing away the insect nibbling above the exposed neckline of his shirt.

'Yeah, plenty of those,' Kat granted, then stood up again to add, 'As far as we can tell there's only us here.'

'No problems with equipment?' Buster queried.

'Nah, unlike when I tried to think up transport in the barn,' Jank grimaced. 'Think and it's here again. Still like Kat said, our defences won't extend past the far side of the paddocks.'

'Which I can't understand. I learnt how to programme them on my last plain and their arsenal had a far greater range than what we've got.' Running a finger over her armlet Kat glanced up at the rapidly darkening sky, her next words more statement than question when she said, 'And I don't believe we were away overly long.'

'No, you weren't,' William agreed, his keen analytical mind having already calculated the time it would take even the fittest of persons to map out an area the size Kat had described.

'Thus, currant defences are back plus our newer benefits, thank goodness to both,' Jannelle laughed.

'Apparently…'

Interrupted by a loud neigh, whatever Kat had been about to say was startled out of existence when the massive Clydesdale tossed his handsome head and disappeared. Replaced less than a heartbeat later by Sophia, a small mauve envelope and a variety of canvas bags.

'Whist least now we know where ye went dinna we, ye smart wee missy. But I must tell ye now I'm in a bit of a quandary. I dinna know whether to celebrate Sophia's return or mourn tha' big boys parting.'

Bending over to scoop up the tiny kitten Annabella answered Mac with a happily chortled, 'I do. Celebrate, perhaps Sophie can morph into any animal she wants or mayhap we might need.'

'I don't think that's possible,' a doubtful Buster negated. 'We know some insects have the ability to metamorphose but to the best of my recollection those of the animal kingdom don't.'

As he elbowed the immense Aboriginal's hip bone Mac growled, 'Will ye two Sassenachs kindly speak the King's English.'

'Change shape,' Jank briefly clarified. 'And is that what she did?'

'What else would you call it? If that's what happened at all... Perhaps it's nothing more than a coincidence Soph found us at the exact moment the horse left,' Michaela blithely commented, and since she was unwilling to waste their remaining daylight answering the myriad of questions she was certain the large Scot was about to pepper them with, leant over to pick up the envelope.

Not sure what to name the faint fragrance which came with the sheet of finely embossed paper she'd pulled from of the sachet, Michaela lifted the note closer to her nose.

'Gumnuts I think,' she guessed before mumbling under her breath when she recognized the elegant copperplate script. 'Home we might be. Home and hosed methinks not so much.'

Perplexed by Michaela's wording, Mac eye-balled the clothing she'd left then returned in before asking, 'Why would you be wearing stockings under those things, wee one?'

'Figure of speech mate,' William grinned. 'You'll have all that sorted out for you later.'

Smothering a blurt of knowing amusement, Jank rubbed his rumbling stomach and said, 'Get on with it, woman, I'm hungry.'

'What happened to thinking?' Annabella lightly mocked.

His, 'Oh yeah, bugger it.'

Coalescing with several guffaws of mirth as the svelte woman passed around the platter of assorted cheeses and crackers she'd manufactured while Michaela began to quote from their latest communiqué.

'Well done team, welcome to your new abode. You've a lot of work to do tomorrow. Study your instructions and please get a good night's sleep. P.S. Watch out for the Mozzies.'

'Bit late for the footnote.'

Fanning her hand to frighten away the gathering of mosquitoes who seemed determined to dine on her slender neck. Jannelle asked the Master Archiver if he had any notion as to where in the structure of the aloft plains they might be.

'Hypothetically, it's a new plain, therefore none but the First to Be and Creator of All should be above. Judging by the flora, equipment and our clothes. Here begins in the early to mid-twenty first century, Australia… Hopefully with all its joys and none of the woes.'

'Wouldn't a Training Plain be better situated above the Assessment Plain?' Jank questioned.

'Mmm perhaps,' Buster said with a wiggle of one dinner plate sized hand. 'Yet that's not the norm. Usually, the newest plain encases the previous ones.'

More interested in what his additional duties might entail than the topic under discussion Mac asked Michaela for the slender rectangle.

'Instructions,' He echoed, his disappointment obvious as he peered into the empty envelope. 'Where's ours then wee one?'

'There perhaps my friend,' Jannelle laughed again as she caught sight of the familiar shapes that had just begun to drift down from the overhanging branches of the Wattle tree behind William.

An hour later a tidy bevy of domed tents formed a half circle behind them as the group relaxed around a small campfire. The aromatic bouquet of cooking meat flavouring the night as their dinner sizzled on the chic heating plate retrieved from the depths of the largest of the ochre-coloured duffle bags.

Cradling a glass of frothy ale and tapping his foot in time to the music coming from his armlet. Mac listened intently as Buster finish explaining the last few rules of the card game that Jannelle and Jank were playing.

'Well done, mate,' Buster said, the younger man having laid his cards down so they could see that the combined value of his hand would enable him to peg out. 'Like I said sunshine, it's a thinking man's game. Thus, if you can play chess, you'll get the hang of Cribbage quicker than a digging dingo.'

'Aye well Bust, that I can. Tha' winters were long in my

village whilst I was growing up ye ken,' Mac replied as he passed Jank the packet of chocolate coated snakes the pair had been competing for.

Grinning at the childish face Jank pulled when Michaela told him to save them for later because they'd spoil his dinner, Annabella wondered aloud whether the fire was safe.

'That's the third time you've asked, and yep, the grounds quite damp underneath and the paddocks are flush with green grass.' Shifting her gaze from the tiny kitten curled up on her chest towards a metal bucket, which Michaela had insisted be filled and placed next to the fire prior to it being lit, then the Billabong Kat added a droll, 'I kinda reckon we'll be fine, as in case it escaped someone's notice, we've heaps of water.'

'Oh sorry, and plus we've got our handy new talent,' Annabella giggled while her scarlet tipped fingers wriggled at Michaela.

Who refused to acknowledge the implied overkill by redirecting the focus of their attention with a curious, 'Annie have you read your letter?'

'I haven't as yet, anyone else?' Annabella choked out between sneezes initiated by a plume of smoke the light breeze swirled into her nose.

'Bless you and not me,' William replied. 'But by the smell of it, foods ready, so let's eat first. We've waited this long so another half hour or thereabouts won't kill us.'

'Tad hard iffen we're as dead as ye keep all telling me we are,' Mac scoffed, then proceeded to use Buster's immense body for a shield when several objects whizzed towards him.

Only the sounds of the bush ebbed and flowed amongst the general clatter of flatware on metal while the companions ate.

96

A colony of frogs serenaded their women folk, whose coy responses vied with the chirping of cicadas and the gentle hoot whooing of owls greeting each other as they awoke from their daily slumber.

Jank's patience had run out as the last morsel of food was lifted from its plate. Whisking the dirty dishes away, he waved his note in the air with a demanding, 'Now,' before tapering his tone to add a politer, 'And whom first?'

'Your mother was here first,' William said, turning towards his soulmate, the faraway expression she wore prompting him to give her hand a light squeeze.

Brought back to the present by this gentle action Michaela filed her meandering reflections away. Picking up the envelope lying in her lap she somewhat absentmindedly reminded William that he, and the other four, had actually beaten her to it.

Then ignoring several versions of, 'But we were asleep.'

A subdued, nevertheless delighted Michaela read out, 'As Ambassadress of this newly formed plain it's your task to welcome any newcomers or visitors and oversee their ethnic requirements… Ah nothing new there. I guess it just confirms we're the meet and greet committee doesn't it my love?'

'Mmm but I've got finance for both on and off plain too,' he replied, showing Michaela the extra line to his letter before peering over the top of her head to grin at Jannelle. 'Chief Justice…Does that mean we're expected to kowtow to you?'

Adopting a lofty pose Jannelle agreed with a teasing, 'Thought you already did,' and clarified her tasks with a general, 'I'm to finalise the nitty gritty of our legal system, stand as adjudicator if required, and when time permits assist Buster with the archiving.'

'When time permits,' Jank protested. 'Will we have any spare time here?'

'You just spent half an hour playing cards before dinner,' Jannelle casually mocked. 'But we'll make it so, for chores and no fun makes bores of us all... Bust, what about you?'

'Pretty much as you'd expect. I'm to delve into the how and whys of the plain but more importantly record the history of how it evolves.' Buster's even, white teeth glimmered in the soft glow of the rising moon when his face creased into one of his brilliant smiles and he chuckled, 'Just my billy of tea and you, Kat? Apart from keeping us safe, does the Chief of Security have additional tasks?'

'Management of callouts.'

The befuddled look which roamed over Kat's face, along with the slight quaver he heard jumping throughout her short response, made the Scotsman bend over to feel the ground around the side of his chair.

Satisfied with what he'd found, Mac lobbed a small pebble towards the young woman and stoutly declared, 'Kitty Kat ye'll be fine, wee one.'

As puzzlement was replaced with glinting steel. Kat caught the small stone in one hand and, without disclosing her final set of instructions, lobbed it back with a crisp, 'Aye James Rory Macgregor that I will, your turn.'

Already free of its envelope, the large Scot pulled a thick piece of red card out from under his cap. Turning it around a few times while he ran over what he'd been able to decipher, Mac handed his closely scripted instructions to Annabella.

'Mmm,' she said. 'The Training Collator ensures everyone's theoretical prerequisites are currant, valid and accurate... Provides training so that the previously mentioned bits adhered to the practical qualifications are met and subsequently maintained.'

Cheeks puffing up then shrinking again in a booming raspberry, Mac's voice was filled with self-doubt when he thanked Annabella then cried, 'I canna figure out what most of the words mean let alone what I have ta do. I was considered a lettered man at home. Yet if this 'tis ye kings English... It's beyond what I was schooled in.'

'You'll be right mate, there's an easy answer to your problem,' Jank laughed cocking his head in the general direction of Buster, Jannelle and his parents. 'We know those four have all had a go at our tasks. Thus, if you don't get it right you can always shovel the blame onto our self-nominated Mentors.'

'Bulldust you can,' Jannelle swore, leaning over to take a playful swipe at his pointing finger. 'Help we will, but it's a new plain remember and we've all got...'

'Chill Wawura the lad's only stirring,' Buster butted in with a puckish grin.

Refusing to answer as she always did when asked what 'Wawura' meant, and shushing Buster as he began to explain. Jannelle closed her eyes and propped her arms behind her head.

The long, pink tongue Buster poked out at her, and his silently mouthed, 'Tell you later,' spread a smattering of laughter around the campfire.

But a longer and louder one responded to Jannelle's, softly sniggering, 'You haven't in the past centuries since we've known each other, nor will you now... Or I'll perhaps return the favour eh, Guni Gabara?'

'Ah, third eye still awake, is it princess,' Buster wryly

conceded, but happily denied her another chance to speak when he added, 'Anything new about your role, Jank? Most of this we've already anticipated.'

'No, not really. The Master Technician is responsible for all computer-generated requirements, communication devises, virtual training games, associated equipment and initially we... I mean I,' he quickly corrected. 'Am first attendee to call outs.'

'Blimey, you probably won't have even a free fifteen minutes, let alone a half hour,' Jannelle grinned, then opened one eye again in time to see the Master Technician reach over one shoulder.

'Who's the man,' he chanted along with the muffled tattoo his patting hand made. 'Who's the man... I aaaammmm the man.'

Fond amusement brushed over his face as William leaned towards Michaela and said, 'Hasn't changed much, has he? I wonder when or even if the rest of our family and friends will be joining us. Jank's not going to be too pleased if he's away from Amber for long.'

'He's a smart man my love. Thus, he's probably got that figured out by now and he doesn't need to change.'

'No one's perfect, Babe.'

'Bro is.'

'Bro's sinless which doesn't mean he gets everything right, mostly, yet not always. Your words not mine.'

'Nearest thing to perfect if you exclude the First to Be and Creator of All,' Michaela shrugged. 'Gosh something's up... They've changed colour.'

'What... Who?'

'Everyone except you, Bust and me,' Michaela groaned.

'Mac's kinda yellowish cream, Annabella's a sunny yellow. Jan's more a pearly cream and the kids are whitish.'

Unsurprised his soulmates physic abilities had once again followed her, William sighed, 'Oooh why not that as well as everything else.'

Her talent in this area had given them a few laughs but also some unpleasant moments throughout their time together so it was a somewhat sour Michaela who added, 'And we know it'll bug me until I figure out what it means, or else it happens.'

Which can be a bloody pain in the butt either way.

Keeping this opinion to himself, William softly reminded his tiny soulmate she usually considered a white aura to be good and pearls too, creamy or otherwise, then raised the volume of his voice to re-enter the conversation with a light, 'Last but never least, you Anne?'

'Oh, I get all the fun stuff,' the flaxen haired woman laughed. 'Administration plus Occupational Health and Safety.'

'Meaning?' Mac frowned.

'I keep all the paperwork moving and for the present, anything of a medical nature will also be directed my way.'

'Well, that's an easy one lassie.'

Her sculptured eyebrows copied Mac's frown as Annabella bluntly queried, 'How so?'

'Och woman, ye ken burn the paper and we're dead, thus nowt need any Apothecaries care.'

Simultaneously rising with Buster to stand on either side of Mac's chair Jank said, 'Okay, update 101 needed.'

While a more formal Buster intoned, 'There are things you must know so you can accomplish all you're required too.'

'Nay, ye said twenty to thirty hours after arriving on a working plain and 'tis nowt been that ye big Sassenach bullies.'

'Twenties just ticked over but I'll hold your hand if you're scared,' Jank snickered as they hauled the procrastinating man out of his seat then aimed his struggling body towards the largest of the tents.

'Nowt scared lad jest a wee bit apprehensive.'

The sound of Mac's jittery burr faded along with their disappearing shapes when the trio of men stepped between the front pair of ropes and entered via the tent's middle zipper.

Finding it vacant of all but a well-padded chair, Buster asked Mac to take a seat and thought, *Portable Archiver, James Rory MacGregor, Scotland, 1822.*

ON PLAIN: GREEN — YET NOT THE ONE EXPECTED

The phrase, *And this ain't the half of it,* silently bounced throughout Michaela's skull like a full volley tennis ball. Trying her hardest to disregard what it may signify in the here and now, she stood up and leaned against the solid protection of William's chest.

'Will…'

'Yeah, I know, Babe… Something's going to happen,' he teased, grinning down into her stormy blue eyes. 'You've just told me that and you had the tone… Mickey the colours were good so it'll most likely be okay. Not one of your bad ones.'

'No… That was different. This is another thing altogether and a strange one, 'cause it feels kinda neutralish, if that's even a word, so… So neither overly good nor overly bad.'

Pulling her into his arms William murmured, 'You'll work it out, you always do.'

'Preface that with eventually,' Michaela sighed and although quite content to stay within the arc of his arms she turned her head to add a louder, 'Show's on, shall we?'

By the time everyone had lined up along the tent's inner walls, the sleeve of Mac's rugby top was rolled up and a small area of skin on his upper arm already sterilized.

Primed for work, Buster lent over the seated man holding a minute gold disc in one hand and a long thin scalpel in the other. While the Master Technician stood just out of range of

Mac's restless limbs, trying not to laugh at the Scot's obvious bout of nerves.

'After I've inserted the disc into your arm and melded your skin back together, you'll feel a cool tingle. Once that's happened put your right index finger into the chamber,' the Master Archivist repeated, nodding at Jank who once again held up a square metal box and inserted his middle digit into its round opening. 'So, you right to go sunshine?'

At this, Mac's already pale face paled even further as he steeled himself for more of what he firmly insisted on calling magic.

'I suppose I should be doing that,' Annabella said.

Pausing to glance over at the svelte woman when his keen hearing picked up her quiet words. There were hints of an ego in his voice when Buster replied, 'It's the first implant on a new plain and I've done more of these than most. Mayhap next time my dear if you don't mind.'

Mac used the rivers of salty sweat that had begun to run down his forehead as an excuse to shut his eyes before quietly demanding, 'Will ye kindly stop your blathering and get ye on with it.'

Happy to comply, a thick trickle of crimson blood wept from the separating folds of skin as the immense man sliced a ten-millimetre cut into Mac's arm. Swabbing the blood away from the small cut, he carefully positioned the disc into place and fused the wound closed.

'And done.'

Startled by the speed of the small operation, Mac peered through one barely open eye at the thin, rapidly disappearing line and blurted, 'Aye ye were telling the truth this time, for it nowt hurt a bit. Man, ye are very good.'

'Like we told you, it's a no pain, no stain procedure, Mr Doubtful,' Buster beamed. 'Now last step cobber.'

Blocking the dark slot with a shaking digit, Mac flinched as a halo of amber light swam out from the boxes centre. Its dull sheen inching past his faint wound before gathering momentum as it rolled across the Scotsman's torso, then flared out until his entire body became fully encased in the wan light.

More minutes than usual crept by while they waited for the amber light to change. But change it did. Amber to bright orange, bright orange to dark green and there it stayed. A green of sorts, nonetheless without the neon vibrancy of the anticipated shade.

'Buster, explanation please,' a tense Jannelle said. 'There's only one colour which symbolises a successful operation.'

'What do ye mean?' Mac yelped. 'Dinna it work?'

Jannelle's lovely face was marred by creases of frowning concern when she softly answered, 'Not as completely as it should do.'

'Never mind, it's not an unprecedented occurrence,' Buster shrugged. 'It just means not everything was passed on. Thus, if previous experiences are to be believed, the practical application will be absent.'

'Annnd?'

The Master Archivist's ebony face creased into a playful grin before he answered Michaela's drawn-out word with a simple, 'We'll might have to teach Mac how to use any equipment invented after he passed over.'

'Aye,' Mac nodded, his nimble mind readily accepting the information pouring into it from the golden implant. 'I really fancy driving one of those jet pack thingy-me-bobs, or mayhap a Lamborghini.'

'Trust you. That car's a very flash mode of transport my friend,' Kat laughed. 'Are you sure you're okay, Mac? Sometimes this part of an induction can make you very ill.'

'Och little one, I've a cast iron stomach. Thus, I'm fine,' Mac bragged.

'Oh yeah? I think not.'

Though she laughed when a click of Jank's finger and thumb resulted in a collage of pasty-faced Mac's and spinning divans being hung on the wall beside her, more than anything, Annabella wished the flux of unanswered questions and warring problems her brain kept producing would either pack it in or else take up residence elsewhere. The few pieces of used equipment easily dispensed with one thought, while her next materialised a well-padded armchair.

'In that case…' Pausing to expel a long sigh of pleasure. Annabella snuggled into the chairs welcoming padding as she added a wistful, 'If you're really okay, Mac, perhaps we should think about going to bed.'

'Aye lass that I am. 'tis like me mind has awoken from a wondrously long sleep. Alas me body's beginning ta feel like I've partaken in a dram or twenty of me Da's home brewed whisky. And aye, iffen that 'tis an offer my pretty one. Give me a few moments more and I mayhap I'll be able ta take ye up on it.'

The cheeky retort made the emerald eyed beauty laugh again yet also earned Mac a definitive, 'No, it was a generic question not a specific invitation good sir.'

'I'm with Annie,' Michaela grinned. 'There's that much running around in my head it's not funny.'

'Before you do,' Kat said. 'I'd like to recap a couple of

things. Firstly, even with the best technical security available, I don't want anyone straying more than a quarter of a click from the Billabong unless participating in an official survey within the aerial cam's boundaries... Secondly; I'm calling for volunteers to man two hour patrols. Jank and I will do the first, Mac and Annabella midnight to two. Buster and Jannelle next, followed by Mickey and Will, then Jank and myself again for the pre-dawn one. Okay?'

'Sure.' Opening the small dictionary she'd materialised to the twenty second letter of the English alphabet, Jannelle dropped it into Kat's lap with a drolly added, 'But methinks Ms Chief of Security doesn't fully comprehend the meaning of the word volunteer.'

ON PLAIN: MASTER

'Hello,' a deep voice of liquid velvet announced once the tent's door flaps had closed behind the exiting quartet.

About bloody time, Michaela thought as she twirled around to squint into the shadowy corner from whence the voice had come. And yet when a tall, smartly dressed man stepped forward all four of the Mentors instinctively bowed or curtseyed.

Perched on the man's left shoulder Sophia was idly playing with a strand of his long, unbound blue-black hair. Her golden eyes not lifting from her game until he shyly requested, 'Please, no need for ceremonies.'

'Welcome, it's about sometime, Bro,' Michaela chided.

'Reproach little one? Will, can't you do something about that?'

The Ambassador's wry expression changed to a comical study of neutrality as he drawled, 'Huh that's your job if anyone's… If you want it done, do it yourself, Master.'

'Chicken.'

Tossing back the long velvet cape he wore as he spoke, Bro flapped his arms up and down. His sudden movements jostling the tiny feline so much, she only kept her balance by sinking her claws into either side of his ears.

'Ouch Soph, don't… It took hours to airbrush out the last lot of holes you put in me.'

'Serves you right, you frightened her.'

Michaela walked over to where their Master stood and stifling a bubble of giggles, rose on her toes to smooth the kitten's ruffled fur. Then used the handkerchief she pulled from the cuff of her sleeve to dab away the droplets of blood seeping from the puncture marks Sophia's sharp talons had gouged in his lightly tanned skin.

'Thanks Mickey, shall we begin?' Four more chairs joined the one Annabella had left behind as the grey eyed man indicated they should sit. 'You're all looking very well.'

'Nice of you to say so... New plain, Boss?' Jannelle asked, impatiently attempting to steer the conversation towards the more prominent concerns occupying her mind.

'Yep, brand spanking new. You all aced the charter test and both scenarios, so...'

'Were they really necessary? And if that was the case, couldn't we have done it the usual way?' Michaela cut him off to growl.

'Which is on a fresh plain?' Bro lobbed back. 'Besides, a bloke's entitled to have some fun, isn't he?'

Bugger it. He's in one of those moods... I wonder how she handles it now, Buster winced.

Better than she used to, William's bemused and rather stunned reply told him. *Now... My lovely wife even encourages him, so I'd recommend ducking if she does.*

It was a rarity for the Master Archivist to be as flummoxed as he felt when William's unspoken thoughts entered his mind. Still only a pinch of time passed while Buster processed it and a beaming smile preceded his laughing, *Wave your hand, then cough.*

If you insist.

Stupendous, the Master Archivist marvelled, a powerful

surge of adrenalin rushing through his overactive mind as he pondered the potential and evidently available benefits of telepathy.

But strong though it was, the emotion departed quicker than it had arrived when Bro's earlier words circled their way back to the forefront of his conscious and he barked, 'You mean it was just another one of your flaming tests?'

'Oh, oh well sort of Bustie. You passed thus don't fret it old man… Anyways you needed to see first-hand how the group would work together. Though Mac's lack of an induction was a twist not of my making. Pity that, 'cause 'twas a good 'un.'

'All right for some. I suppose it's something else you'll just dump in a glitch file?' Jannelle tartly griped. 'And thus, it didn't count as an official call out?'

'No, an informal one.'

'Then why bother at all?' Michaela snorted. 'We could've spent the day rounding out our first line of business not fardling about in the sodden mud.'

'All training's important even at your level of capabilities. Seeing your people manage and I might say, excel, in difficult or unusual situations should bring a smile to anyone's face, including you three whiners.'

Rethinking the curt words tottering on the edge of her tongue when Bro added a filament of iron to his last four words. Michaela replied with a saccharine sweet smile then thought a note pad onto her knees and a pen into her right hand.

'Having observed our teams past twenty-four hours. Is there anything constructive you wish too, you know, tell us?'

Bro laughed but ignored the tiny woman's sugary tone to ask William if he'd ever noticed how tetchy women, and especially his lady, became when tired.

You're gone no matter what you say mate, Buster warned.

Not so, William declared, silently rising his hands to form the universal keep me out of it sign.

'And that's a correct call my love,' Michaela sniffed. 'You're way off base if you think Will's gonna fall for that one, Boss.'

'Wow, golly gosh, this is really riveting stuff. Hope you don't forget to file it Master Archivist... Moving right along here Master mine, let's kindly skip the chit chat and get back to business.'

'Okaaay, Jannie. Obviously, Micky isn't the only irritable one. Thus, housekeeping now, new stuff later.'

Cutting off Buster's disappointed objections with an abrupt horizontal slide of his hand, Bro made a point of looking all at four before the last twist of his head left him gazing directly into Michaela's eyes.

'Mickey, you managed your first tasks as Ambassadress somewhat well. From the moment you arrived until we came together just now you undertook your duties with a seemly outward calm and a smile on your face, well most of the time anyway,' he said. 'Although...'

'Although...?' Michaela cautiously prompted, wondering if he was still just trying to get a rise out of her, or whether she really missed something.

Answered by a basin of steaming water, fluffy hand towel and the cake of soap which materialised a few inches above her lap.

Michaela hid the wave of relief that skipped over her body with a snippy, 'Oh, I get it. Somehow, it's my fault that overgrown, red haired barbarian didn't want a shower,' then blinked the offensive articles away with a smugly admonished, 'I asked Bro, and I'm dammed sure you know that... Don't you my dear little spy?'

'Hey, that's a bit harsh. It's not as if you were discussing state secrets or the like.' Belatedly realising he'd blurted out the answer to Michaela's smug question, Bro matched her grin and laughed, 'Anyways, as Jannie asked, moving right along here. Will my friend, as usual you supported Michaela by following her lead without too much hesitation. Your trust in her outweighing any reticence you might've had, thus thy predetermined tasks were also carried out with your normal aplomb.'

'Kind of you to say so,' William said, shaking the hand Bro extended while adding a firm, 'And my wife did ask.'

'Aw I'm merely joshing folks, merely joshing,' Bro grinned. 'Now Buster... You correctly surmised the costumes, weaponry and continent of the physical plain scenario all without aid from the archives. Also very well done, although...'

Buster's bushy brows joined together as he frowned and, like Michaela's had been, with a guarded tone parroted their Master's, 'Although?'

'Although... Mac nearly shoved you through the wall you know.'

'Bulldust like that was ever going to happen,' the enormous man scoffed. 'Could've taken him with both hands and feet tied up.'

'Elsewhere maybe but here? 'Cause my oath he's quick on the uptake.'

'Crappola like I...'

Once again Bro cut off Buster's half-finished complaint

with a grin and wave of a long, almost feminine hand as he twisted sideways to smile at Jannelle.

'Jannie my sweet. Your role as Chief Justice has yet to be utilised. However, the mammoth change in your acceptance of the unsubstantiated more than justifies my confidence in you.'

'Buuut?' Jannelle felt compelled to query when the man lent over to lightly busk her cheek with his lips.

'No althoughs or buts for our Chief Justice or Plain Ambassador,' Bro laughed, holding up the silver flask he'd taken off the belt of his finely tailored trousers. 'Drink anyone?'

Unhurriedly taking several swallows when the quartet declined his polite offer. It took Jannelle's loud clearing of her throat to jolt the man into resuming his summary.

'Oh yeah sorry, where was I? Um, the other plains conception have normally been a need generated occurrence. Once an existing plain nears full capacity eight souls are charged with the task of preparing a preliminary staging ground for the next one.'

'Jeez, Bro, we know all this,' Buster yawned.

'Nothing like a refresher course,' Bro said, sending the now mock-snoring man a look full of playful dismissal. 'Who determine what the purpose of the plain is to be and write a Charter which the plain's personnel must abide by. Five of my Dad's senior Helpers are given the names of the persons considered for each role. Once the selection process is finalized and the chosen ones have completed a round of scenarios, currently of my design…'

'You said…'

'Scenarios Jannie, I only made up the scenarios,' Bro cried over the top of Chief Justice's on-going comments. 'I didn't know about Mac not having been with us before… Honest. That was Dad or perhaps Mistress Fate, not me.'

Confident his last sentence would stop the exotic looking woman arguing further, Bro ended his synopsis with a hurried, 'They need to survey the environment, produce living and working facilities, determine what if anything differs or needs more research i.e. Here you've got telekinesis.'

'Materialisation more than telekinesis,' Buster contradicted. 'We don't actually move things from one place to the other, just think them up.'

'Must they only come from someone's fertile imagination?' Bro shrugged. 'Questions anyone?'

'Only about a million,' William frowned.

'Or two…' Also frowning again as he slowly stood up to stretch on the off chance some movement would ease his stiff body and their Master would finally get the hint that they were dammed tired even if he wasn't. Buster's innate curiosity trumped the weariness of his immense body, its itchy force pushing him into a reluctantly blurted, 'So why the envelopes, oh Humble one?'

Their master's shout of glee rolled around the nylon walls of the tent, however the four's less than impressed faces saw him spin it into a light cough then say, 'Telepathy is what your team brings to the table. Please remember that… The envelopes are a way to steer you in the right direction, oh and to remind you of me.'

'To the first, Will and I have already connected and thus have some of that figured out already. The rest of them may take a bit longer but I doubt it will be much,' the Master Archivist grunted.

'As to the other…' Jannelle hurriedly added. 'Once met

or heard of, never forgotten.'

All humour had fled from their Master's face when he sadly murmured, 'It's been known to happen.'

'True, but they were bloody fools dear one,' Michaela stoutly proclaimed, extending her palm upwards to blow him a kiss. 'And of course, doesn't refer to anyone here.'

'Wouldn't bloody well want to,' Jannelle snapped before leaning forward to address Buster and the bombshell he'd so casually dropped into the conversation. 'You have? Where, when and what does it mean?'

'Here, now and I surmise this is the first plain where telepathy will be a day-to-day tool instead of the whimsical by-product of DNA. blending like on the current physical plain... And I'm predicting that at the moment only the four of us might have this particular ability?'

Noticeably brightening Bro corrected Buster with a happier, 'It's six on this plain counting me and Dad, 'cause we can talk to anyone who wants to chat. Otherwise, you might be right... Well for now anyways, since this is to be the Training Plain... Isn't that what you all wrote first?'

'You could've joined us instead of eavesdropping. A five minute meet and greet wouldn't have killed you... And when you say scenario was it a genuine call out like from our previous homes or what?'

'Mickey everything you did on the physical plain was real. Kat felt a lad's soul come to us again and one of the men you aided, who might've died if you hadn't been there, significantly helped determine the course of the war.'

Unconvinced Jannelle muttered a brief, 'Sophie and the horse? How does that fit?'

Scowling at the woman, fatigue saw her words come out

curter than intended when Michaela cried, 'Look enough already. You two told us what was going on. Therefore, one would presume you already know the answers.'

'So, cease presuming and start listening,' Buster bluntly reprimanded. 'We do what we're told, same as everybody else, plus it's a big leap to say we knew what it was all about. They chucked us into the cement mixer same as you.'

After staring at Michaela through half-closed eyes for a moment Bro demanded to know whether she had or hadn't felt safe.

'I did. I don't lie and my gut told me it was safe. Anyway, as you'd expect, I knew Jannelle as soon as she spoke.' And as the final stream of memories escaped from the vault sunken into the soft tissue at the base of her brain, Michaela glanced back and forth between Jannelle and Buster to add a provocative, 'Aloft and on the physical plains. Besides it had to be Buster since there's no one as humongous as he is, this side of the Neanderthal Plain.'

'Discounting Buster,' Jannelle shrugged. 'It's that one particular conversation we had which flourishes first.'

'Hardly ever any more. However, as yoooou brought it up...'

'Dammit,' Jannelle groaned around a smothered yawn. 'You sure can hold a grudge.'

'Dammit... I sure can,' Michaela contemptuously snorted. 'Could've been so different. Should've been so different, and the result would've been... Most likely so much better.'

Opting not to verbalise the rest of her recollections any further. The Chief Justice became the pointed recipient of tiny woman's angry, toxic snarl.

'Ah no ladies, I don't think so.' The desire to divert the

116

two women from their ancient quarrel, which usually ended in laughter, yet was a topic they'd discussed ad nauseam in his opinion with or without the exotic woman's presence, saw William's arm skate around his soulmate's long neck. The firm hand he covered her mouth with an effective silencer as he asked, 'Bro, how long have we got until we're expected to be operational?'

'First official Induction is in three months.'

Gladly following the man's transparent lead Buster said, 'Jumping jellyfish that's early, and our companions Master... Have any of them they met you in person and if not, when?'

'Noooo not in person, but I reckon it's gonna get pretty interesting here, so I'll be around. Hence I'm bound to bump into them sooner or later.' Breaking off to tap the side of his nose with a long finger, Bro whispered, 'Still, till it's happened mums the word, okay? Now before I go there's one other little thing that I'd like to point out...'

'Oh, for Pete's sake,' Jannelle mumbled around a flurry of yawns. 'What now?'

'Miss Kat... Bro's house?'

'Oh,' Jannelle said, the hand she'd used to smother her yawns with then dropping to prop up her chin as she looked inward. 'Sorry missed that one Bro, the security bit I mean...'

While Michaela yanked William's fingers away and grouched, 'Kat graciously accepted our apologies and we got here, didn't we?'

'Forgiven Jannie, yet Kat had it well under control which she so eloquently told you, and is something it wouldn't hurt you guys to remember... As to you short stuff,' Bro grinned. 'I had supper laid on for you at my place. You were supposed to say...'

'Don't you think it worked out better the way we did it?' Buster cut in to ask. 'Especially, since you insist on being invisible to the others.'

'Actually, I was thinking about getting to know them there. Buuut nonetheless next time…'

'Buuuut nothing, obviously either works or we all thought "Home", which would be a hell of a coincidence,' an unapologetic William also butted in to say. 'Apart from the supper that, knowing your abilities or rather lack of in the kitchen, was probably either microwave stuff or straight from someone else's freezer. What's the problem and as Jan mentioned, Sophie and the Clydesdale?'

The silence following William's remarks grew and continued to grow until the grinning man disappeared. Leaving only the kitten and a mauve envelope in his freshly vacated chair.

Michaela slumped back into her seat and with a deep expulsion of air peered around the tent to quietly smirk, 'Didn't have an answer for those did you, oh not so Smart one… Just more fardling envelopes.'

Smiling ruefully when Bro's light titter entered his mind, and by the exasperated expressions his companions now wore, theirs too, William said, 'This could be the best three months in history.'

'Or the worst depending on what else might come our way,' Buster sighed, letting out an almost inaudible whistle as he read the note enclosed within the envelope.

'Oh, bloody oath, dare I say it… Now what?'

'It says, Miss Jannie, 'You know who and where you came from, but the rest?' And I'll bet three boomerangs everyone except Mac is Aussie born and bred.'

Since he'd spent his original life dwelling in the smallest of Australia's states William laughed, 'Well we knew that, so no takers big man but I'll go a step further and add predominately Tasmanians.'

'All of whom still sit under the umbrella of the Australian flag,' Jannelle murmured as she stood up. 'Mind, I know what you mean... Tassie's pretty special.'

'And our red-haired mate?' William said with raised eyebrows. 'His accent's pure Scottish.'

'Yeah, he's Scottish that's bleeding obvious. But regardless of that irrefutable fact, his language and history disc started in Van Diemen's Land 1850 not Scotland 1822 where he was born,' Buster softly ruminated. 'Thus, he's either sailor, crown employee, free settler or mayhap a convict.'

ON PLAIN: JANK, ANNABELLA, KAT AND MAC

Scanning her bracelet's security programme and finding all as it should be, Kat walked Mac and Annabella down to the campfire. Jank catching up with the three as they stopped to gaze into its dying embers and the muted sounds of the late evening settled around them. The rustle of unseen animals moving through the undergrowth an eclectic harmony when linked to the light breeze which rippled across the Billabong causing the inky water to strum the softest of beats as it rolled against the sandy shore-line.

'It's lovely here isn't it. We really are the luckiest of souls,' Annabella said before raising her eyes to take in the beauty of the star dotted sky. 'What else is out there, Kat?'

'I'm not an experienced gardener but the paddocks look pretty lush to me and there was a faint hint of salt on the breeze,' a quietly jubilant Kat said.

An avid fisherman since early childhood, Mac wondered how soon he'd be free to indulge in his one of his favourite pastimes. The thought a pleasant distraction from the grimmer of the day's events and added a vagueness to his, ''Tis bonny news about yon sea yet ye dinna see nay animals?'

'No… There's plenty of scat about though. Mainly kangaroo and wombat. Oh, and the odd snake trail or two.'

'Mmm, they like that type of scrub. But I'm really glad we didn't see any,' Jank shuddered. 'And the lack of animals was strange considering the time of day. Normally the roos would gather around the water holes before sundown.'

'Our presence would probably stop them using this side of the Billabong to quench their thirst,' Kat said. 'However, they aren't too skittish if you keep a reasonable distance. I would've thought we'd have seen a few inquisitive ones grazing or at least drinking from the other shore. So anyways, it'll happen or not and are you gonna be okay, Mac? I can do your stint for you if you'd prefer to pass tonight?'

'Nay lass, dinna fret ye self. Mind, whilst our wee conjuring tricks 'tis a bonus, tha' dying part 'tis nowt but a bummer,' the Scotsman joked, letting out a short bark of laughter followed by a far more sombre, 'Ah, there's an awful lot to comprehend with this plain business. Ye filled me in a bit on how the world had gone, and whilst the progress of technology was horrendous to see, methinks a man coated in burning oil 'tis still a lot worse. And I canna help thinking that even with the disc implant I'm nay going to be much help ta ye any time soon.'

'You'll be fine. Besides you don't have any choice cobber and neither do we,' Jank said before patiently recapping what they'd told Mac the previous evening. 'Once on a working plain, you can stay there for eternity. Apply to live in another era like most eventually do or, as our circumstances seem to indicate… You can be moved on if the higher ups feel you'd be better utilized elsewhere.'

As his head began to slowly nod. Mac recited Jank's latter sentences several times to ensure he wouldn't forget them. Nor the wary air of respect the younger man had displayed when uttering his last remark.

'Going into a different era can be a complex business,' Kat

121

crisply stated once the large Scot's head had ceased to move. 'But we'll have to go into the nuances of that another time. You two should get some sleep and we've a perimeter to check.'

Keeping to an even jog, Kat headed towards a narrow animal track which barely divided the thick undergrowth as she ran over her mental checklist.

Personal protection gear, water, energy bars, First Aid kit, weapons, both the plains and my own.

Confident she had all the necessary equipment under control the petite blond stopped just short of the foot wide path.

'Let's do a gear check,' she said, making a half turn to find Jank's long muscular body lit by a tunnel of moonlight. 'You know where the armoury component is?'

'I'm more a lover than fighter but yeah, it's in place,' Jank replied, pressing the symbol of a light blue dragon etched into the side band of his armlet. And when he touched the symbol again, an almost indiscernible change of colour convinced Kat his clothes were once more coated with a shield of liquid armour.

Sturdy footwear had replaced the sheepskin Ugg boots he'd worn to dinner and attached to the narrow belt looped through the top of his trouser-clad hips; a well-crafted scabbard housed a bone handled knife. Include an automatic handgun, water bottle and his own personal medical kit Jank appeared well prepared for whatever they may encounter.

'I think I'll do,' Jank said, a cheesy grin of compliance planting itself on his face as he pre-empted Kat's request to spin round and executed a near perfect pirouette.

Without commenting, Kat checked the weight of his hip flask then, ordering her shoulder lamps to switch to a low green beam, stepped between the twin lines of shrubbery. Walking in single file neither spoke again until the end of the track opened out onto the wide strip of paddocks.

'Jank… Just because we can't die and might not feel any pain on this plain doesn't mean we can't be disabled.'

She preaches to the converted, Jank thought, recalling what he'd said to Mac earlier that day whilst tugging on her long, blond plait as hard as he could.

Eyes blurring with tears Kat swung around, her momentum adding extra force to the clenched fist she retaliated with.

'Oooof ouch.'

Backing away from the furious girl Jank rubbed his aching belly and gasped a rueful, 'You pack quite a punch and I reckon that answers pain 101… We both felt it didn't we?'

'You think… Hold him, gang.'

Surprised more than worried by the strong hands that now gripped his upper arms Jank kept his gaze firmly locked with Kat's as he cried, 'Oh, stop it. You know who I am.'

'You might know who I am yet what about your other rellies? How's the memory?'

'Ditto sweetheart.'

The weapons pressing against my spine couldn't possibly penetrate my body armour, Kat winced, swinging her head around one shoulder then the other. 'Well, like, like, I'll be dammed… Let him go.'

When Jank voiced similar words and directed an affirmative nod towards the three souls standing behind her, the knives were removed from Kat's back and his arms freed.

You're doing Missy Fate, or planned? Jank mused. *Whichever, the folks are going to love this.*

It had been decades since they'd last met, but of course he hadn't forgotten any of them. Kat and a tall, olive-skinned youth were the youngest cousins from one side of his extended family, their companions the eldest on the other.

So when Kat coolly announced, 'The Chief of Security thinks it's time for some straight talking... And perhaps reintroductions are required?'

Jank was unable to stop his lips twitching into a wry smirk before he quickly retorted, 'Talk yes, as to the other, I don't think it's necessary. The guy with the pink hair is Alb, your biological brother.'

Shaking the teenager's hand, Jank turned to hug the dark haired woman standing beside him.

'Bubbles, you're looking lovelier than ever and to pile coincidence on coincidence, here's Norman,' lightly patting Bubble's older brother on his shoulder, Jank finished with a laughing, 'You mayhap recall Amber, Killy and Nimble.'

Stocky of build and several inches shorter than his sibling. Nimble enveloped Kat in his arms. Giving her back a quick pat, he released her to bow towards his wife and sister-in-law.

With greetings exchanged, Kat pulled Jank to one side to quietly question, 'How and when did your merging happen? If that's what you call it?'

'Yeah, oddly enough we do, which is more than weird. They woke up when I went to bed last night and we merged out as the tents were being set up... Although if you mean initially, it was on the Assessment Plain. You?'

'Assessment Plain then prior to dinner yesterday. Norm spent most of his free time after our initial placement scouring

124

the Archives. He found records of your coming aloft but nothing about where you'd gone or if anyone else could merge and separate like we can... Not long after we moved to our previous plain a note was popped under our apartment door saying I was to front until further notice. And that's also unbelievably strange considering nobody would openly accept our relationship... K.A.T apparently stands for "Kin All Together". Norm hit the books again hoping to find the owner of the seal the letter was stamped with whilst the rest of us spent ages trying get an interview with our plain's Secretary of Assessment.'

'Ah, I'm guessing that didn't go to well,' Jank grunted.

'Like it surely didn't. Nothing but a bloody waste of time... How do you decide who fronts you?'

'We take it in turns and unless one of Buster's protégées happens to be our plain's Archivist, we've always found the archiving methods haphazard if not completely inadequate. Do you merge much?'

'Four heads are better than one, so on call for sure. Otherwise, we stay demerged for as long as we're able too.'

'Ditto again and merging can be pretty handy for assessments.'

Rather startled by this Kat said, 'You don't explain first? Sorry I always thought you were er, somewhat strait-laced.'

'We try or tried to tell 'em. Isn't our fault nobody wanted to know that the recent Assessors keep putting bunches of miserable sods, whose ego's way exceeded their capabilities, on the same board or councils.... Who subsequently were too stupid and unimaginative enough to believe us. Either way it defied any sort of rational understanding considering what we were capable of achieving,' Jank smugly replied. 'They wouldn't believe us nor the evidence of their own eyes. Thus, it serves 'em right if we worked the system. That's what happens when you consistently group moronic piss-pots together.'

'Mmm and like you, we did try,' Kat said. Then freed her cynical side in a hard put, 'Admittedly not for overly long after we'd been told to shut up a few dozen times. Nonetheless try we did and with prayer, cosmic mores, crossed fingers or like you said, Mistress Fate… Between us we aced everything.'

'You forgot natural aptitude,' Jank augmented. 'And look where that got you, so no slacking off on this plain, little Ms Chief of Security.'

'Errr no, therefore it's past time the parameter got re-checked. We can chinwag later and thank you; the mantle of Chief of Security will ease somewhat now we've got more helpers.'

Stepping forward and waiting until there was a lull in the conversations going on around them, Kat announced, 'The Billabong is approximately one kilometre round and it takes a quick paced five minutes to span its circumference. Buddy up, we go right first… If you're not in security gear kit up now.'

'We know all that. What do you think we've been doing while you lot lazed about,' Nimble teased. 'Plus, we merge out in whatever the front happens to be wearing.'

'Us too,' Kat replied with a minute nod, the only reaction she showed on hearing this titbit of uniformity while she studied the outfits her two cousins and their wives were wearing. 'But like you said Jank, we're obviously deemed pretty dam good at this security business or else we wouldn't be here. So why haven't we seen you before?'

'Stealth mode,' Amber said, vanishing then reappearing

with no more than a twitch of her nose.

'When it comes to talents like this,' Killy explained while her outstretched arm came and went with every upward vee of her wriggling eyebrow. 'Once our front has the ability the rest of us usually manage to do it too, merged or not.'

'And so, say all of us,' Norman revealed while his lower torso blinked in and out.

Trying to contain her laughter as different pieces of the group's bodies came and went. Kat asked Alb to take point position.

'Like we now know,' she warned. 'On this plain we still feel degrees of pain, thus I'm thinking we'll also suffer the consequences if harmed. Stay alert, weapons at ready. Move out.'

Pink hair now hidden under his woollen beanie, Alb did as requested. The thick grass of the paddock muffling the tread of their boots leaving only the buzz of insects and occasional growl of a Tasmanian devil to disturb the deep silence of the night.

As the pair of white gumtrees earmarking the entrance to the paddock side of the track came within range of her keen night vision, Kat walked the last few metres then waited till her companions were loosely grouped in front of where she stood, before disrupting the friendly peace they'd completed the last half of their loop in.

'Spread out more this time, six or so metres between pairs,' she ordered. 'Oh, and study the terrain again for reference points, you won't always have a full moon to walk under…'

Her attention caught by a stream of shooting stars that suddenly lit up the mountain shadowed horizon, Kat paused until the last particle of light completely disappeared then added a dry, 'Yes, and like I said, you'll most likely be tested on it in the next few days... Norman you and Amber on point. Jank with me please.'

Jank folded his arms across his chest and slouching against one of the enormous trees casually groused, 'This is all a bit melodramatic, isn't it? Mum said she felt completely safe here and you've got nearly all the latest modes of armoury so why the night hike? I for one, do not need the extra exercise.'

'Do you know where we actually are?'

'I know as much as you.'

'Which isn't all that much is it? In all honesty we could be anywhere. Just because some of us feel safe here, myself included, doesn't necessarily mean we are or always will be... Notes and everything else aside this might still be just a flopping convoluted test scenario. Especially, when you add the stallion into the equation. Signs mayhap indicate otherwise but until I'm fully convinced, we're not taking any chances. Oh, and speaking of which, I thought you kitted up before we left the Billabong?'

'Sophia most likely explained the horse business...'

'Animals don't morph or appear out of nowhere in any era of history that I know of.'

'Well, I dunno about the animal switcher-roo stuff, and holistically speaking is the rest really that important in the here and now? Annnd, since you're the one who checked me over, little Ms Chief of Security. Was, or wasn't I? How's your hand?'

'I... No, I suppose not,' Kat sighed. 'Though elsewhere it'll be handy. And that's Chief or Madame Chief if you don't mind. But while I admit my hands sore, I'd bet my next glass of wine your stomachs worse. The liquid body armour in your clothes should have stopped me hurting you, ergo it wasn't activated.'

'Ah yes, however it was. You tested it yourself Chiefie, Chiefie.'

'Don't ever do it again.'

'What? Do what again?'

'You pulled your bloody body armour,' Kat said between tightly clenched teeth. The disquiet she felt at the risks he seemed so willing to indulge in forcing her to step forward. Close enough to tap her nails on the hard coating of his upper torso she added a chastising, 'That was flaming stupid and dangerous. What if...'

'I knew who everyone bar Mac, who I'm pretty sure I've met somewhere, was as soon as I woke up... Plus I've been ninety-nine point nine per cent certain we're where we should be since the moment we landed back.'

'Bro's home, a new plain as we've been led to believe, or somewhere else? Choose.'

'I suspect Bro's complex is where we were last night and this morning, even though that's not necessarily the truth either buuuut... But I don't see the point in it all unless we're on our new plain. Before we left the war zone today, I just thought home and somehow I reckon everyone else must've as well.'

Glancing skyward in time to watch another shower of stars light up the skyline Kat murmured, 'Actually, I didn't... But until we're sure, a hundred per cent sure that is, I think it prudent not to mention our, er strange abilities to anyone else for the present... Okay?'

Curious to know what Kat would consider sufficient proof

Jank asked, 'We've got all the mod cons, as Annie called it, and we can all materialise things out of thin air which none of us could do prior to being here. Therefore, what exactly would it take to convince you?'

Not really sure herself, Kat hesitated for a second or two till her well-founded confidence surged to the fore.

'Dunno, but regardless of the where or when,' she grinned up at him, 'We probably couldn't be better prepared security wise... Conversely, you're on first and final caution, mister. 'Cause if you ever pull your body armour again whilst on deployment, test scenario or nay, I'll bury you in soooo much slimy faeces you'll choke on the bloody stuff.'

ON PLAIN: THE BILLBONG —
ANNABELLA AND MAC

'Bossy ain't she, for such a little thing,' Mac fondly observed as he produced a double float couch and two earthenware mugs. 'Coffee and perhaps a wee natter, my lady?'

'Mmm yes please, and Kat's got a lot of responsibilities, plus people relying on her here,' Annabella murmured, waiting until he'd joined her and the deeply padded divan had stopped rocking before taking a sip of the steaming beverage he'd handed her.

Finding the whisky flavoured coffee very much to her liking, the svelte woman drained most of it before she spoke again.

'Are you sure you're really all right, Mac? Even with all the information I got from the implant, having to accept my death and work everything out nearly sent me nuts.'

'Did ye have aid, pretty one?'

Smiling at his compliment, Annabella's tinkling laugher echoed out across the water.

'I did indeed, my Mentor was my closest friend and confidant. Still, it took a few weeks for me to feel at home there.'

'Then what? Ye just swanned around playing the harp and such, did ye?'

'Would that be so bad with the right person?' Annabella lightly flirted.

'Nay lassie that would be fine for a wee while. Yet ye should ken, all play and nay chores, makes James Rory MacGregor a bit dullish.'

'You dull? Somehow, I doubt that's ever true… And since everyone is eventually required to contribute to their plain's day to day workings. Combine it with any personal study or community service you may wish to participate in, you may well find yourself busier now you're dead than you ever would've alive.'

'Ah well, that's good, but there's room for some fun too, eh? Tha' tasks may be a calling but I've a yen ta hold someone soft in me arms. Would ye consider a dance with me wee one, iffen that's nay to bold of me?'

Annabella nodded her consent as the sounds of a spritely reel replaced the plain's night-time symphony. Waving their mugs away to wherever manufactured items went, she stood and slipped into Scotsman's beckoning arms.

Some twenty minutes later, a breathless Mac guided Annabella back to their seat. Relishing the coolness of the light breeze as they sat down, he looked at her flushed face and surprised himself by thinking, *Apart from the stabbing pain I feel every time the picture of me wife and clan flashes before me inner eye, this dying business is nowt all grim.*

The implant had dissolved the majority of the gaps his lack of normal entry omitted, leaving his avid curiosity awash with questions and instilling a fierce desire to explore the many periods of the physical and aloft plain's history that were now available to him. So, as he eased his long body into a more comfortable position, he asked Annabella about one of the first things he'd decided to do when the vast wealth of knowledge from the disc had sunk its tentacles into the centre of his brain.

'Will you teach me to drive, lassie?'

'Methinks driving shouldn't be a task you practice in the dark,' Annabella laughed, yet in less time than a flutter of her eyelashes would take, a wooden table with a variety of small, remote-controlled vehicles sitting on its unvarnished surface materialised in front of them. 'However... You can certainly play with these.'

A World War Two tank sat next to a bright yellow beach buggy. The red, white and blue flag fluttering at the top of the recreational vehicle's antenna, almost identical to Mac's own clan's coat of arms. Beside it squatted a dark blue quad bike, then came two modes of transport which would make many a person's heartbeat quicken. A black Harley Davidson and the sleekest of sports cars, a red Lamborghini.

Needed or not, Annabella quickly explained how the controls functioned and couldn't help but smile as she watched Mac's hand hover over this one, then that one, before scooting back to the beginning of the line. Placing the miniature tank on the ground he thrust the control toggle forward, and chortled with childish delight when it went grumbling along the beach.

Once he'd had a brief practice with each, Mac added a definite whiff of challenge to his, 'How about a wee race, lassie?'

A corresponding look glimmered in the emerald depths of Annabella's eyes as she softly taunted, 'Sure you're up to it, Mac? I'm thought quite an expert on a couple of the plains.'

'Is that right wee one? Therefore, ye won't be above making it a tad more interesting, will ye?'

'Oh lord,' Annabella laughingly spluttered as she watched the red Lamborghini grow to its natural size, the body of the

133

equally luxurious, silver Maserati she'd opted for matching it in sleekness if not length.

'Thrice around tha' wee pond, lassie?'

'Fine... Three, two, one, go...'

Two twin beams of light pierced the tree shrouded darkness as the deep roar of revving engines filled the night. Mac's red beast the first to cross the line he'd drawn in the sand, while the Maserati remained never less than an inch behind it.

Gearing down to round the sharp southern curve of the Billabong, Mac chanced a quick glance at his dance partner. Momently distracted by the shimmer of her silky, flaxen hair, he missed seeing a protruding tree root. It's small elevation enough to send his powerful vehicle carolling into Annabella's.

The shrill screech of metal on metal only just preceded the continuous blaring of damaged horns as both cars slammed into the belt of shrubbery heeled trees at the far end of the beach.

The unexpected sound of throttled back engines, so closely followed by the crunch of folding metal, brought the four in the tent to their feet in a wave of concerned fright.

Michaela's, 'Circle up,' lost in the shrill shattering of wood and the whooomp of igniting fuel.

'No ones in there,' Annabella cried out as the quartet of Mentors appeared outside the largest of the tents.

'Aye there're nowt but wee toys, ye ken... 'Tis my fault I put Annie up to it,' an almost repentant Mac just as loudly proclaimed, slowing his stride so he could grasp hold of Annabella's chilled fingers when he drew close enough to actually see the expressions on their faces.

Shading her face from the heat of the burning mass, Michaela wavered between laugher or letting loose with a frustrated scream. But her due to the palpable disapproval of her fellow Mentors and Buster's disgusted, 'Bloody morons... '

To which he added a verbal blast of what sounded like Aboriginal profanity. The tiny woman decided it shouldn't be the former and firmly banked the desire to shout out the latter.

Quickly self-organising, a storm of foam attacked the pungent pyre as Kat and Jank broke through the undergrowth. 'What the hell... '

'No need for the gun Kat, no one's hurt. These idiots... ' Shouting to be heard over a loud explosion of crunched leaves William's head rolled left with an upward thrust of his chin then right with a downward jerk. The grimaces of the errant pair standing on either side of him explained by his repeated, 'These idiots were just playing.'

Though not doubting William, Kat's shoulder laser remained primed, and Jank asked to do a survey of their immediate surroundings.

'You got that Alb? We'll be back shortly. Out.' Ending the hunched over coughing fit she'd used to hide her quiet murmur when the bracelet on her wrist responded with three green flashes. Thought became deed as Kat straightened up again and aimed her own spray of foam towards the burning wreckage. 'Why don't you like, you know think it away?'

'Because it nowt damn well works,' Mac complained.

'Really? That's odder than odd. Like how come Michaela? Everything else is super easy.'

'Oh, because Br...' Swiftly adjusting her slip up Michaela shrugged and said, 'Er someone says so I guess.'

'Some consistency wouldn't go astray,' Jannelle sighed

before raising her eyes to the blue-black sky as if expecting to find their Master's face peeping out from behind one of its brilliant stars. 'Try again someone. Even when it's out we won't want the mess it'll leave.'

'Already have, so just circle up,' Buster ordered. 'Merging may overcome what a singular mind can't.'

Coming up behind Kat in time to hear what Buster had said. Jank uttered a droll, 'There speaks the truth of it and we're good,' into her ear.

With united hands and concentration saturating each countenance. It took only a few seconds for the crumpled mess to evaporate, taking any smouldering trees and underbrush with it.

Slapping high fives all-round, although the companions viewed the rapidly cooling ground with satisfaction. As the burst of adrenalin coursing through their bodies dissipated, it was obvious they were all to one degree or another feeling the length of their first day together.

'Coming to bed, Babe?' William whispered against Michaela's cheek while his arms crept around her waist.

'Mmm think so.' Tipping her head to look up at Mac, then quirk a questioning eyebrow at Annabella. Michaela's starkly added, 'If the fun's over for the night, we're going to bed. I put forth that the 'might've beens' can wait till we gather for breakfast,' and lighter toned, 'Kat you all right?'

Was answered with several nods and Kat's, 'Yeah thanks, everything's as good as we can make it.'

'In that case, goodnight, everyone. Jan, Bust see you at four.'

Ambling next to his partner in crime as she walked back towards the waning embers of their campfire Mac took hold of Annabella's elbow.

''Tis a bit late to go to sleep now do ye not think… Shall we play a wee bit longer afore we do our bit on the boundaries?'

'No improvising, okay?'

'Ye chicken wee one?

'No, but we've just dodged a bullet and somehow I don't think we'll get off so easily if we do it again.'

Hidden amongst the sweet-smelling leaves of a tall gum tree, the First to Be and Creator of All, Bro and the golden eyed Sophia watched over the small cluster of tents, their ongoing vigil continuing while the newest plain's citizens left for their separate destinations.

Keeping her heavy-lidded eyes fixed on the shadowed figure creeping along the otherwise pristine sand of the opposite shoreline, Sophia snuggled further into the warmth of her Master's lap. *Good day, oh Sinless one.*

Yes sweetie, it's been a very good day, a relieved Bro smiled, lifting the silver vessel held in his hand towards the partly leaf blocked heavens. 'To the successful beginnings of the last known plain.'

Several hours later the yellow strands of the breaking dawn had begun to caper between the fronds of the tree before a yawning, Bro said, 'Ah, night shifts over guys.'

'Thou art correct yet stay a moment longer,' the First to Be requested.

Withdrawing his hand from the side pocket of his long white robe, the ageless one attached the smallest of golden bells to Sophia's collar and handed a minute chest of similar hue to his only child. 'For a task if not free of concern, nonetheless also well accomplished dear ones.'

137

ON PLAIN: BREAKING OF A NEW DAY

Standing on the edge of the sloping southern paddock, Kat had been enjoying the peace and sweet, crisp smell of the awakening day when the faint sound of a twig breaking behind her made the petite blond swivel around, a weapon appearing in one outstretched hand a Nano second before her drink disappeared from the other. But it was only Alb, Norman and Bubbles, who lifted hands in mock fright as they trod the remaining few metres of soft grass between them.

Aware of how seriously her merge mate took her fronting duties, Bubbles quickly apologised for the miss-step which had caused the young Chief of Security's heartbeat to quicken. Yet far happier it was her merge mate and nothing more sinister, Kat waved away the willowy girl's admission of guilt. Artfully twirling her gun around her finger a few times, she slipped it back into its holster while thinking a tray loaded with a variety of beverages into her other hand.

As he took hold of the one closest to himself, Norman voiced the question each had mulled over throughout the night.

'Are we going to tell them or shall we play the 'Keep Secret' game for a bit longer, Chief?'

Even though she'd been pretty certain the question would be asked, Kat was yet to find an answer she felt they'd all be comfortable with so there was a touch of wariness to her quietly replied, 'Jank and I will remain the face of the merges and for the present, publicly it will only be the two of us. It's not my preferred option yet there's still a hell of a lot we don't know about this place. Thus, slow and cautious, it is. At least until an entire survey of our security arc can be done and we get to know everyone. And you're all to remain invisible unless you're alone with Jank's people.'

'Caution is good Kat, but nay if you're wrong. It could take months if not decades to regain their trust,' a contentious Bubbles stated. 'Keeping a momentous secret like this to ourselves mayhap have extremely adverse effects... And what about Will and Mickey, surely you don't doubt them?'

'I'm reasonably confident they'll understand the need-to-know basis, as will the others, and if I'm in error then I'm in error,' Kat replied with an undertone of growing anger.

'What if they decide to be peeved at the lot of us?' Bubbles lobbed back, her willowy body swaying as her feet jigged from left to right on the dew drenched grass. 'We don't all agree with this.'

'No, however we've all signed a contract that clearly outlines that, regardless of the situation, whoever's currently fronting has veto rights,' Alb shrugged. 'Irrespective of what the majority opinion maybe.'

'Yes, but in this instance in particular, if Kat's wrong everybody here may suffer from the backlash.'

'Bub mate, you know I'll take the blame for any mistakes I make when I front, like as long as I get the kudos too,' Kat retorted.

Loudly humming the opening bars to an ancient surfing song.

Norman only stopped long enough to say, 'Kudos, if merited that's a given, and you sure will get the blame if we turn out to be right. Remember when she made us go bloody surfing… We nearly drowned.'

'Oh, for poop's sake shut up,' Bubbles cried. 'Dead's dead and you knew better than to merge out. Especially since we were, A; on a damn surfboard and B; in public, but nooo that didn't matter to you. Idiot that you are, you're the one who spotted the piece of eye candy and decided to strut your stuff. We've told you tonnes of times, we consider it your stuff-up, not Kat's.'

'Wouldn't have happened if we'd gone to the cricket like planned,' Norman momentarily ceased his humming to contest.

'Oh, shut uuup.'

Heartily sick of the tune and as weary of the dated argument as Bubbles was, Alb put an arm around her shoulder and with a friendly squeeze said, 'Both of you shut up and must I remind you for at least is the umpteenth time. It took a while for us all to figure out how to handle the merging… This aside seen or unseen, the eight of us were all there yesterday.'

'Shut up yourself… And I might have missed a bit, 'cause I fell asleep a couple of times,' Bubbles ruefully confessed, glowering over at her now silent brother to add, 'Norm you know Kat was told what she was doing here… Anyways at the very least she's fixed it so we're well armed thus I doubt anyone will be able to find a really valid reason to criticize.'

'Now I'm glad you've sorted that out, Bub,' Kat laughed.

'Damn that's twice in two minutes.'

Blowing aside a strand of her long, dark ponytail a rain of tea scattered in all directions as Bubbles threw her hands askew. They didn't travel very far, yet it was enough to admit she was aware of her predisposition for debating both the yin and yang of any topic under discussion.

Barely managing to dodge the rain of hot liquid coming her way, Kat swung round in time to see Jank and his merge walk around the large Boobialla bush which almost surrounded the western white gum and had kept the foursome hidden from her line of sight.

'Hi, we've been er, reviewing our position here. Therefore, if you're agreeable to it, we'll keep the merging to ourselves unless necessity dictates otherwise.'

'Heard all that Kat. Argue much do you?' Nimble enquired. 'But like Bubbles so succulently said. What about honesty, trust and all that sort of boring crappola?'

'Annnd as she also said,' Alb stressed. 'With a secure parameter arc plus our first night here done and dusted without mishap... Well apart from the cars...'

'...No one can really complain,' Norman finished for him.

But preferring William and Michaela to be told if not the rest of the group Amber replied with a short, 'Oh really?'

Unwilling to justify her decision again and aware that despite any ongoing differences, her merge mates would think nothing of spending the next ten years defending her viewpoint, the young Chief of Security sent the trio on the next circuit of the area.

'It'll be easier with just us, so if you wouldn't mind, bye-bye, Nim.'

Under no illusions as to what his cousin referred to Nimble scoffed, 'Whoa up a bit missy. We operate under the democratic republic system. So, I'll merge when I damn well please, if I damn well...'

'Later, my love.' Even though Killy had paired her brief interruption with a sharp tug to his hand, the mocking stare she sent the petite blond made it abundantly clear Kat was the only

141

intended recipient for the challenging taunt in her briskly added, 'You can enjoy hammering out the finer details over a brew or too.'

When Jank's shoulders rose then fell in a shrug of compliance, Nimble held out his other hand to Amber while Kat chose to scrutinise the open grasslands until the Master Technician emitted a quiet moan.

'You too, huh? It might have some beaut benefits,' she said as she flinched at the ashen whiteness of Jank's face. 'But I'll be glad when someone discovers a way to merge without all the bloody grief that goes with it.'

Too narrow for the pair to walk side by side, the animal track leading back to their campsite was smooth and well worn, the beams of sunlight that streamed through the branches of shrubbery allowing them to keep a steady pace as they revisited the previous twenty-four hours.

'I do remember you all,' Jank said. 'You were a feisty little thing at times and a credit to the family. So, stick out that stubborn chin of yours as often as you like and remember regardless of our personal opinions, there's now at least seven of us who've got your back.'

'Oh, trust me I will thanks, and to borrow Nim's fine word, crappola, sometimes our bickering drives me nuts… Do you have the same problem or are you a tad more civilized?'

'Until we learnt to merge and unmerge whenever we wanted too it was a bit dicey. You know women,' Jank chuckled, which ended abruptly as he inadvertently dropped his head to one side.

'How do you get away with saying that? The boys would turn my grey matter into a sieve if I implied something so sexist, fronting or otherwise,' Kat quizzed over her shoulder.

142

'Trust me he doesn't.' Amber's soft, distinctive voice flowed forth from Jank's mouth. 'Hence the ducking, eh Babe?'

Extremely pleased her merge were yet to have that particular ability Kat lightly swore, 'Blood oath, they can enunciate aloud when merged? Perhaps I haven't got it so bad after all.'

'Yeah, and while it's usually fine I've found it pays to be cautious. Funnily enough our ladies acquire a fetish for high heels and bikinis when they haven't enjoyed what we've done when in charge...'

'Plus, they don't give a damn where we merge out either,' Nimble muttered.

'Oww shame.'

This time it was the sound of Killy's voice that Kat heard. However, apart from a few giggles, she refrained from speaking again until the last thicket of trees before reaching the Billabong's sandy foreshore could be seen.

'Undoubtedly, there's more to learn about this extra talent of ours.'

'You think,' Jank said. 'Once we're better organised, we'll take the time to study each other's merging idiosyncrasies. And yes, until then, be it right or wrong, mum's the word.'

ON PLAIN: MEETING ROOM OPENING —
ONE WEEK LATER

William stood beside the open doorway of the newly completed meeting room, patiently waiting until the last of the chatter died away before lifting the lid off a long rectangular box. Bowing with courtly elegance he offered the contents of the satin embossed receptacle to his soulmate, who curtseyed with similar grace then rose to remove a pair of rune-etched scissors. The Ambassador's fingers wrapping themselves around the tiny woman's as she lifted the pewter cutters into the air.

'We, the first Ambassadors of this the last known plain hereby declare this wondrous building open.'

The duo's arms had begun to drop with their last syllable. Levelling out with the rainbow-coloured ribbon strung between the arched door furniture, only the slightest of pressure was needed for the shears twin blades to sever its silken length.

Over the top of several rousing cheers came Mac's exuberant, 'Right gang, funs over. 'Tis time to git ye wee butts inside and git ta work,' as he leapt up the newly tiled steps dragging a laughing Annabella behind him.

Yeah, that's enough pomp and pageantry, Michaela groused, rather put out at the abrupt ending to what in her mind, was an important first occasion.

Hush Shmich. Remember humour is often a disguise for

grief... And he's still grieving for his kin folk little one.

Her sudden ill humour fleeing as the warmth of Bro's velvet baritone walked into her mind, Michaela quietly replied, *Sorry, Master, I humbly apologise. Will you be joining us on this auspicious day?*

I'll be around if you need me. Still why... Would you?

Still why... Would you? Michaela chorused whilst trying to block out the last of her thoughts. *Dammit, now what.*

Stop swearing, go and enjoy yourself.

Hey telepathy 101. A bit of privacy please, Michaela chided. *Besides something's gonna happen isn't it... I can hear it in your voice.*

I can, she repeated. But the warmth of her Master's touch had gone from the tiny woman's mind. The remnants of its cooling exodus overlapped by the contents of her wary thoughts.

William wondered what had put the distracted expression on his soulmate's face but refrained from saying anything until the remainder of their small company had passed under the arced lintel of the hall's main entrance.

'Care to share, Babe?'

'Was it noticeable?'

'Probably only to me. You weren't 'away' so to speak, for more than a few seconds.'

'Oh good, um I was a bit peeved at Mac that's all and... And...'

'And?'

'Bro picked up on it. So, I got an empathy reminder,' Michaela softly sighed. 'Oh, and something is going to happen again, soon too. I'll bet my next cappa on that.'

'Ohh, yet once again your tone tells me it's an okay

145

something, thus can be left for the present. We've got things to do and remember we're amongst some very gifted and intelligent company,' William advised, grinning down at her when Bro's knowing snicker poked the soft tissue of his outer brain and by the way she screwed up her nose, Michaela's too.

One of the last to enter, Buster had halted in the middle of the large hall to sniff at the sun-kissed air.

Jank's curious glance prompting him to inhale again before saying, 'I love the smell of newly cut wood, don't you?'

'Huh, far better without the blisters, thanks very much,' Jank sourly replied.

'Yes, I expect so. Ah well, not to worry we heal quickly enough.'

Jank's, 'Fine for you to talk,' earned him a consoling pat on the back from Michaela when she and William walked past the two men, heading for the table and chairs at the far end of the room.

The trials of the last week had certainly challenged them. Their collective and individual skills having confronted then overcome a myriad of problems. Some small, some large, however it was the scare they'd had the previous afternoon which now made the tiny woman shudder.

Gathering for a late lunch in the northern paddock the group had relaxed for the first time in days. Thus, with her inner self refuelled, Jannelle had wandered up the rocky outcrop which quartered the field.

Regrettably, lost in the splendour of the emerald foothills and contrasting purple hue of the mountains ranged behind them, she miss-stepped. Her tumbling fall and the string of vulgarity spewing from her mouth bringing their short respite to a frightened end. The sight of the ivory shinbone, glistening with blood and torn skin that protruded through the lower half of her trousers stunning them all.

Mick honestly, I'm fine, Jannelle said, a broad smile creasing her face when Michaela snapped back to the present and her eyes swung in the exotic woman's direction. *There's no harsh pain here girlfriend,*

Still mate, you keep an eye on it...

'If you two have finished your little chat, can we get started?' Kat asked, wishing her telepathic abilities were as strong as the Mentors appeared to be.

'You'll get there, mate,' Jannelle replied. The young woman's questioning look making her hurriedly add, 'How did you know anyway?'

Even though he'd been the first to enter, Mac was almost last to sit. The grating noise his chair made when he dragged it away from the table, competing with the raspberry he blew when he plonked himself down then scoffed, 'Och woman, ye aren't normally as blank faced as ye are when nattering in ya heads ta one another.'

'The ever so vacant expressions you lot have been running around with are a dead set give-away,' Annabella added.

'Aww shucks, just add it to the rest of the stuff we've yet to rock,' Michaela grinned. 'Anyways welcome everyone. It's an honour to be here with you, but prior to commencing today's forum I'd like you all to join me in a toast.'

Without needing any more than this to be said. Chairs were pushed back and the crystal glasses that had been evenly place around the oval table raised towards the ceiling.

'By unanimous decree we name our plain Talaa, the Training and Lifestyle Academy for the Afterlife.'

Brief though the Ambassadress's salutation had been, the

147

significance of its content caused an emotion charge silence to fall over the small population of the newly named plain.

Lasting only long enough for the eight to resettle themselves, the Chief Justice ended it with an appreciative, 'Mmm nice, where'd you find this?'

'I seem to remember someone acquired the expensive taste for it on a visit to an early Celtic period, then over-indulging more than a few times on down time,' William replied.

The wriggle of an index finger in his soulmate's direction and the glowing colour of her cheeks clearing up any possible misunderstandings as to whom the Ambassador's sly jesting was aimed at.

'True, yet it has both pleasurable and naturally medicinal attributes. Nor was I exactly alone either, was I Mr Tag-along?' Michaela sniffed. 'But I do admit to the extravagance of the brew. For even aloft a purchase of this size consumes a truck load of boons. Though since we only have to now think to produce, its cost free and easily replicated.'

'Oh well bugger it, that's arse about face. Produce as much alcohol as wanted yet have to erect of our buildings manually,' Jank sarcastically grumbled as he shook his red, blistered palms under his mother's nose.

'For now, young Jank, for now. Everybody's working on tha' wee concern and ye aren't the only one sporting war wounds,' Mac said, placing his own scratched and bandaged hands on the polished strips of Blackwood that had been laminated together to form the top of the table.

Michaela sympathised with them both but not wishing to be diverted by a rehash of their various wounds, lightly banged the gavel William had whittled for her, which successfully

148

brought that area of the conversation to an end before it could stray any further.

'Recorder on, Anne?'

'From the onset.'

'Thank you.' Although it wasn't really necessary Michaela looked down at the first line of their agenda then around the table before saying, 'Item one: Discussion of known variants of telepathy.'

Putting his hand to one side of his mouth, Mac leant slightly to the right and whispered a purposely noisy, 'That means who can do what, don't ye ken,' against Jank's ear.

'What I'd like to know…' Pausing to re-enforce the coolness of her over-riding question with an icy glower Jannelle added, 'Is how you lot managed to get so much done in less than a week?'

'Hey, we worked sun up to sun set every day, plus some,' Kat chided. 'If you've got any complaints…'

'No complaints, not a one. Still considering the limitations you were under how were you able to do this much in just the last few days?' the Chief Justice asked, spreading her arms to encompass the high, vaulted ceiling and the intricately panelled walls of the meeting room.

Annabella felt her normally placating nature dissolve under the weight of Jannelle's rather caustic words. Because regardless of the how, the building team had worked so hard and whilst she may not be sporting any blisters, she certainly had plenty of splinters and more than a few aching muscles.

'If you wanted to know that you should've stayed and helped instead of gallivanting around the flopping countryside,' the svelte woman sniped with her own shot of icy displeasure.

149

But it was the loud slap of hands on the table which really forestalled the rest of the Mentor's questions. Kat using the downward movement as a thruster to push herself into a standing position.

'Jan's actually on the right track,' the pretty blond calmly announced. 'I'd like you to meet the rest of us.'

And though Kat's pre-arranged cue came earlier than anticipated. Jank quickly stood with a briefly posed, 'Plus mine.'

'Aye, ours too,' the Master Trainer stated.

He and Annabella barely making it to their feet before the faces of the four conspirators whitened and, with shimmering auras and shaking bodies, twelve more souls slowly oozed from their bodies.

Told you something was gonna happen Will, was the first thing that flew from Michaela's mind while she altered her look of astonishment to a purposely harsher mien. For hard though it was, the new souls being either members of her and William's family or long-time friends, the fact they'd chosen to keep this to themselves merited a far more serious reaction than the tingling delight which flooded over her. *Easy does it for now guys. Let's see what Kat has to say for herself before we rip their bloody heads off.*

'Chief of Security explanation please.'

Surprised, but refusing to be intimidated by the temperature of Michaela's voice or the aura of burning anger that radiated off William and Jannelle, Kat expanded the table. Materialising a dozen more seats, she signalled for everyone else to sit.

'When we, as in me and mine, gathered on the Assessment Plain we were able to physically merge into one body. At first

150

it was only Alb and me.' Pointing to the pink haired teenager then the other two members of her merge. Kat's thoughts back peddled to the earliest history of her merge as she added a slower, 'When we bumped into Norman about a month later, he'd already merged with Bubbles... I was fronting when we met and so was Normie.'

Doffing his cap in an attempt to lighten the mood of the room Norman laughed, 'To be precise she knocked me "a" over "t".'

'Yeah, and as I helped him up, we... Well, we like merged into one another and have been able to at will ever since.'

'Do you have to stay connected at all?' Buster broke in with one of his beaming grins.

Grateful that at least the immense man didn't seem to be adversely perturbed. Kat returned his grin with a shaky smile.

'Well to date, any more than a couple of days without remerging makes us a bit ill. I mean at least it did on our last plain, here we really haven't...'

'Haven't had much energy left for experimentation. You know, too busy building meeting rooms,' the willowy Bubbles butted in with an acerbic glance at Jannelle.

Who returned it with an equally cutting one of her own as she arrogantly touted, 'Well I was right wasn't I? Took more than just the flaming four of them.'

'Dammit, we should've been told,' Michaela cried. 'This is a very special, er, ability to have kept to yourselves.'

'They're both right,' William frowned. 'Don't you think we could've used the extra hands when we went off plain?'

'I tried, it simply didn't work,' Jank curtly replied. 'We mightn't have been aloft as long as you three but we're not brain dead either.'

'Huh, that's extraordinary debateable,' Jannelle snapped. 'And you're actually expecting me to believe you didn't think it important enough to tell us?'

This time it was a clenched fist that crashed down onto the tabletop. Kat using the silence she'd bought herself to stare at each Mentor in turn before unapologetically admitting, 'The subject came up but as Chief of Security I opted not to… Would you like to meet everybody else or not?'

Well, would you? Or are you just gonna sit there whinging… I mean like we mentioned our telepathic capabilities before Jannie's accident or Bro's more than normal input here, Buster berated the three Mentors in disgust. *This is brilliant, cut the kids some slack.*

Brilliant of course, but we bloody well should've been told, Michaela swore. *Besides mum's the word about Bro in case you forgot, oh Smart one, and it was a unanimous vote that opposed explaining the telepathy business any earlier.*

Yeah, plus Mac and Anne are to flipping old to be called kids, the Chief Justice added.

Not to mention the rest of them. Although he too, was delighted on personal level, William couldn't fathom why they hadn't been informed prior to now. *In fact…*

In fact, nothing, Buster all but yelled. *For pity's sake shut it or I'll get the Boss to shift you off to Herd Island for a century or two.*

'Excuse me. If you're finished with your private conversations?' Kat said as she rapped the table with another tightly clenched fist. Whether it was her anger-tinged delivery or the extra-long emphasis on the word private, when her three protagonists eventually smiled, though none as widely as the beaming Master Archivist, the petite blond nodded to Jank.

'Nim and I were siblings on one of the physical plains. We'd already merged with our wives when we met up, which coincidently was also on the Assessment Plain,' the Master Technician began, putting his arm around Amber's waist before hooking a thumb at Nimble and Killy. 'Like Kat, as soon as we touched, we merged. Annabella?'

Squaring her shoulders and running unusually moist hands down the sides of the figure hugging, navy shift she wore, Annabella tucked a stray strand of hair behind her ear and slowly got to her feet again.

'Sorry, perhaps we should have told you,' she said. 'But since that particular ship has sailed, please welcome my merge mates.'

Of the three who had flowed from her shapely body Dutch, a clean-shaven, broad-shouldered man whose reddish blond hair was swept back into a long plait, was the tallest of the new-comers. Beside him stood William's father.

A handsome man, wiry of build and sporting a fine shock of thick white hair, T. Thomas, held onto the hand of a hazel eyed beauty. Tall for a female, shards of silver were liberally sprinkled through her dark, upswept hair. Both an ideal frame for the strength displayed on the shapely woman's pale, serene face.

Never one to seek the limelight, Bettany smiled at William then with a short heartfelt, 'Sorry son,' quickly sat back down. And whilst the men hurried to join her, Annabella started to explain the strange beginnings of her merge.

'On guard duty the first night after we came back. I had the eerie feeling we were being watched and kept hearing voices in my head...'

'Who doesn't?' Michaela piped up without thinking.

153

'Yeah, who doesn't? But come on, then what? This is totally, unbelievably fascinating.'

Buster's encouraging words and beaming smile saw Annabella add a bemused, 'Well…Well as I've always talked to myself. I thought with everything that had happened in the previous twenty-four hours I'd just gone a bit loopier… That is until I tripped and landed flat on my face. I felt so ill, and for a second or dozen had a real battle keeping my stomach from tossing out everything I'd eaten that day. But before Mac could help me up, my merge mates were squatting next to me. Crackers or nay I was completely bamboozled.'

Swift to contradict her Mac said, 'Iffen ye are loopy… So 'tis the rest of us and ye dinna look too out of sorts wee one. In fact, ye looked as cool as those long, green thing-a-me-bobs we had for lunch today.'

'Cucumbers, and thanks nonetheless I was, and pleased as I was when I recognised them, well bar Dutch because I hadn't met him that often. I really did think I was going bonkers.' Allowing the spot of laughter that followed time to abate, Annabella hugged herself tight and ended her tale with an up-beat, 'And even though I'm totally comfortable with most of it, like I said, you two would've kept me from sprouting a few hundred grey hairs if you'd been more forthcoming.'

While she smiled at the playful finger Annabella wagged between Jank and herself, the petite blonde's explanation was a firm and concisely put, 'I clarified everything when you reported it to me. Then considering none of you even knew you'd merged, which is another anomaly we've yet to puzzle out. Would you honestly expect me to have discussed something like this with you?'

Fully aware they'd breeched the boundary of the Mentor's

trust; Kat also rose to her feet again. Driving home her most salient points with sharp, plainly understandable, gestures.

'We've only been here a week and until an entire assessment of the security arc area is done, I have, and will, use every tool at my disposal to keep us safe.' Elevating the thumb of her raised fist as she found her vocal stride Kat began to count, 'One; we didn't, still don't, know whether this isn't or wasn't a series of test scenarios. Whatever it might be, your safety is my primary responsibility.' And while the thumb of Kat's right hand extended into a parody of her left, she added, 'Secondly; are we merely participants in a variety of peculiar call-outs or perhaps as we've been led to believe, settling a new plain? Thus, I say again, our safety is my principal task and lastly... Not everyone has the authority to be as well informed as your Chief of Security should be.'

Almost choking on the last huge gulp of air inhaled, Kat pulled in her thumbs instead of thumbing her nose at the lot of them like she'd fleetingly thought about doing. The round of applause which erupted from the merge mates coloured her cheeks a rosy pink, and since all the Mentors promptly joined in, she tapped the top of Mac's head.

Quick to take the hint, the Scotsman jumped to his feet, the man's beckoning fingers urging his merge mates to join him.

Gathering the small, goldish-brown haired woman who'd been sitting beside him into the centre of his chest, Mac's eyes never left her tear drenched face when he lent back to say, 'Och how I've missed ye all, my bonny wee Irish rose.'

Neither of the final two souls, both appearing to be in their mid to late thirties, spoke while they stepped behind their chairs to hold out their arms to their clearly overwhelmed Clan

Chieftain.

Taking his time to pull out a well-used tissue, Mac wiped his nose then embracing all three proudly exclaimed, 'Good ladies and gentlemen, I'd like ye ta meet me clan. Gohal, Mharrissah and my lovely wife Julz... And wheest, up till forty minutes ago I dinna have a notion they 'twas even with me.'

ON PLAIN: HOW MANY?

Sorry she'd missed the opening ceremony Sophia raced through the doorway of the meeting room. The tap of her nails on the wooden floorboards barely slowing as she reached the table and clawed her way up its closest leg. Sashaying into the middle of it, her golden eyes widened in surprise when she saw the extra souls sitting around the table.

After sending Bro a quick, *Interesting developments my way oh Curious one, come look.*

The tiny puss curled up next to a water decanter and with deceptive idleness, licked away the stray drops of moisture trickling down its side.

Waiting for Mac's merge to re-seat themselves, and another round of beverages to be dispensed, Buster also cast his mind out, *Thus we're now the tribe of twenty.*

'If you've got something to say, could you please speak aloud,' Kat growled as she stared from Mentor to Mentor. 'At least in public.'

'Ka...' With broad nostrils flaring one of Buster's hands plucked the envelope that had stopped him mid-word from the air as the other slid his belt knife out of its leather sheaf. Making short work of reading the piece of flimsy, bright green paper it contained he said, 'How many?'

As she vocalised the lightening quick conversation still raging between the four, Michaela said, 'Twenty-three, there's twenty-three of us.'

'You counted Sophie, Mickey?' Annabella asked.

'Nay that twill be only twenty-two iffen ye include the stallion. And in that case why not four like us ye wee scamp?' Mac grinned as he scooped up the tiny feline. 'Mayhap there are four of ye as well, thus that would make two score and four.'

'Two score and five methinks,' Michaela corrected. 'Two score and five.'

'How so Mum?' Jank challenged. 'Four of you, four each of us equals twenty, plus maybe another four for Sophie only adds up to twenty-four... Leastways it did when I went to school.'

'Aw sorry, maths never was my strong point,' Michaela replied between tightly clenched teeth. The soft bag of laughter Bro dumped on her brain making the scream of annoyance teetering on the cusp of her tongue all the harder to swallow.

'Aye, even iffen Sophie merges out to four 'tis still only twenty-four,' Mac counted out. 'I dinna think I want ye to be doing me accounts lassie.'

'No Dad, every time for that one mate,' Jank slowly replied, directing a piercing look of scepticism towards his mother.

Dammit Bro now they think I can't even count. You won't make things easy will you, Michaela criticised, yet was unable to stop a small smile lift the corners of her mouth when the other three Mentors chorus of dry, *You thinks,* skated into her mind.

Leaning forward so she could see everyone Michaela allowed her smile to widen as she mumbled aloud, 'Ah well, no matter how many of us welcome everyone,' before loading the table with more snacks and bottles of water.

'Ah, thanks for this Mickey, but we really can feed ourselves,' Annabella laughed. 'The merge mates have the same abilities as the fronts do.'

'At least to this point,' Jank added, helping himself to an Anzac biscuit then dipping the edge of it into his cup of tea.

Once their short respite ended it was William who said, 'I know we all feel the following critique essential to the evolution that will take this plain to its fullest potential. Teamwork, Training, Duty of Care, Rostering and Housekeeping being the critical aspects we've chosen to make Talaa known for...'

Continuing on as if only an intake of breath had occurred not a change of speaker Michaela added, 'Five essential elements that must be mapped so everyone may enjoy the fruits of their labours, expand personal pathways, and attain the level of expertise required of them which will safely take us into the next millennium and beyond.' Then with a smile of joy glowing in her eyes, she held out her hands to the ones sitting next to her. The final set of fingers around the table intertwining as the blended voices of the last known plain chanted, 'Talaa... Training and Lifestyle Academy for the Afterlife.'

Losing the wonder of their connection as the circle of hands slowly disengaged. Michaela found her eyes drawn to the tiny kitten scrambling her way up William's chest.

The wider plateau of William's shoulder always seemed to be the intended end of Sophia's rapid climb, yet Michaela didn't think what occurred when she'd got there would ever have been on Sophia's bucket list. The second of her back paws only just touching the shelf of bone when an aura of pearlish silver suddenly surrounded the puss's tiny body.

As Sophia shimmered and shook, the pitch of her gagging screams rose till the orb splintered into a pile of crumpled stars. The last tumbling down William's back as Sophia vanished, ousted to heaven only knows where by the arrival of a miniature Emu chick.

Surprised, though by now they probably shouldn't have been, none around the table moved until the delicate bird flapped his short wings and, with long neck extended, launched himself into the air.

'No, don't sweetie,' Annabella was the first to cry. 'Emus can't fly.'

But it was too late, for undaunted by the worry that had flecked Annabella's light tones. The tiny bird skilfully avoided the reams of digits that flew out to catch him. Safely landing on the table, a mere second later he also began to shimmer and shake. Soft feathers morphing back to black fur, the Emu chick once more supplanted by the silky coated feline.

Somewhat tentatively reaching out to caress her old friend. Michaela nearly missed Jank's, 'Bro, Mum you added Bro. He's the twenty-fifth.'

Looking over at him, Michaela involuntarily straightened when the area around the rim of her peripheral vision lightened and Bro's liquid velvet voice poured from her between her parted lips.

'Yes oh, let the secret out of the bag why don't you, Clever one, she included me. Sometimes I use your mum if I can't be there myself, don't I, Mentors?'

'Indeed,' Jannelle firmly stated. 'Master it would make more sense if you simply appeared.'

'Sorry, I'm not able to do that just yet. Thus, this will have

160

to do.' And as the volume of Bro's deep tenor began to fade, they strained to catch his final, 'You're all doing really well... But it's less than three months to first Induction kiddywinks, so time to get a wriggle on.'

'Don't go,' Jannelle called out. The lonely sound of her plaintive words echoing off the wooden rafters making her slump back into her chair as she forlornly lamented, 'Dammit Michaela can't you keep him here?'

'You know better than that and how busy the man is,' Michaela reminded her. 'Anyways he usually raises more questions than he answers. As I suspect this plain of ours will do. So, back to business.'

'No,' Jank sharply disagreed. 'Obviously, you four know Bro personally while I'm thinking the rest of us may only know of him?'

'Yes, like you just witnessed, and I'm pretty damn sure you already knew Jank, Bro uses Michaela as a conductor to speak as him or for him from time to time. The Mentors have all met and worked with Bro in person, your turn will come,' William stated with an off-hand shrug. 'Besides I'm sure if you search your memories our Master has used her to communicate with you prior to your arrival on Talaa.'

'Hey Mick... That must make you a receiver-transmitter geeky freak,' Buster grinned, which quickly faltered when a hard kick was fired at his shin and the tabletop vibrated under the impact of being hit with William's open palm.

His face had turned the colour of sour milk while an ice burg finalized every syllable as the Ambassador snapped, 'Michaela isn't nor has ever been a freak you bloody fool. Never again do you hear? Never... Again... Speak about my wife like that. This has followed her throughout her life on her physical plains and to some degree aloft, but that type of thinking stops now.'

Angrier than he could ever remember being, William rose from his chair and stalked to the window. His flattened palms beating out a drum roll of anger as they pummelled the wall on either side of its wooden casing.

Just as swiftly leaping to his feet, three long strides placed the Master Archivist within touching distance of the furious man.

'I'm so very sorry, Will. That was very remiss of me,' Buster apologised. 'Jannie has the right of it... Socially inept and unfortunately sometimes my mouth jerks into gear before the diesel's properly warmed.'

'She is so much more than that... So much more,' William muttered, lifting his head to stare up into Buster's worried brown eyes as he once more reiterated, 'Never again.'

'No, never again.'

The gentle touch to his bare forearm saw William sweep his soulmate's slight frame into his arms and allowed the ferocious rage that had encompassed him to slither from his rigid body.

Almost a minute of tense silence followed before the Ambassador felt controlled enough to turn them all back to face those seated.

'In this instance,' he began. 'Duty of Care must come first. It's one of our primary elements. What my lady believes. What we wish to be known for... And it's everybody's responsibility to always remember it.'

Having placed an arm around each of the pair's waists, or almost in Buster's case, William slowly levitated them back to their seats. Where he reached up to plant a none too gentle fist on the edge of Buster's purple clad shoulder and mimicked Mac's broad brogue to quietly add, ''Tis right clever that ain't it? Our wee troop have been a practicing too, dinna ye know.'

A busy five hours later, Michaela stifled a yawn and formally addressed the shrunken group for what she hoped was the last time that day.

'Thank you again for the way everybody's pitching in. It's awesome the speed we're evolving at, isn't it?'

'Aye well, try peeking at it from our perspective lass,' Mac grinned. 'We have ta listen to them plus whoever's talking.'

'You'll get used to it mate…' Though his mouth turned downwards there was more than a glimmer in his eyes when Jank finished with a thinly disguised, 'It has its definite advantages in a more private sense.'

Wanting nothing better than to have the meeting ended so she could revisit the day within the privacy of her mind Jannelle smirked a short, 'Tsk, keep it clean, cobber,' then a more formalized, 'In summary we've agreed to the following; each resident, on a rotating basis, must undertake the basic chores required to maintain the living standards of Talaa, and within a seven-day period each shall undertake ten hours of on or off plain community service. Personal development to be assessed on a three-month basis. Any forthcoming Inductees are to be housed within the base complex for a minimum duration of twelve months. One hour of physical exercise per day is mandatory for all souls, meeting adjourned at nine pm…'

While the Chief Justice paused to have a sip of water. Michaela laughingly grunted, 'And by the end of next week we want somewhere better than tents to live in.'

163

Peering at her from over the blueprints scattered across the bottom end of the table Mac grinned, 'Aye soon wee one, soon. Though ye idea of roughing it is nay alike mine.'

So much to do, Jank groaned to himself as he escorted Kat out into the waning orange rays of the setting sun and headed for the Billabong. Determination quickening his steps as he contemplated the past few hours, what they had entailed, and wondered how on earth they'll manage to get everything done within the rapidly shrinking time frame.

'To work,' he said, in way of a farewell when the tannin-stained water came into view.

'Mmm I imagine Dutch and Mharrissah will be glad their shifts over,' Kat replied, quickly thinking herself out of the gown she'd worn for the meeting and into her work gear before waving a sketchy goodbye as she picked up her pace to jog past him.

Not stopping until she reached the row of tents, still arranged in the half circle behind the unlit fire pit, Kat cast her mind inward. Her face blanching as her merge begun to flow out and she fought to detain the nausea bopping about like a bunch of drunken worms at the base of her throat.

'Normie, you and I'll take the next shift. Bub and Alb have some tucker then hit the sack.'

Looking at the extra whitish hue of his front's face Norman calmly countermanded her order with, 'Duty of Care Kat… You know we could hear everything thus no graveyard shifts for you tonight.'

Alb, spying the mutinous line her jaw had taken, lightly mocked her earlier gesture when he held his hand up and with thumb also extended stated, 'One; you've been flat out all day so rostered or nay, you're not going out tonight. Two,' he added as his other thumb flipped upward. 'It's the Chief of Security that's going to be needed tomorrow, which is you and only you, in case your sleep deprived mind forgot.'

'And thrice; we're here to help, ye ken. We're forming a clan remember young missy and ye should know by now ye dinna have ta do it alone,' Mac whispered against Kat's ear as his large thumb also wiggled in front of the petite girl's nose.

With a rueful grimace Kat grabbed the offending digit, then sagged back into the warmth of the Scot's muscled chest to mutter a resigned, 'Hey, who's in charge here… You or me?'

But the concerned faces of her merge mates plus the tactic nods of the others when they gathered around her, saw Kat revise her plans with a weary nod of thanks.

'All right I cede to your people power… Alb divide everyone except fronts and Mentors into shifts covering tonight and the next twenty-four hours. I'll take it from there tomorrow.'

With a short nod of farewell Kat wound her way through the small crowd, politely asking her trio of merge Fronts to walk with her. The sound of her brothers clearly directed instructions slowly drifting away as they strode down to the edge of the Billabong.

Hands thrust deep into the side pockets of her cargo pants, Kat turned her back to the dark waters. Then with her tone now as inflexible as her rigid body she looked at her three cohorts in turn before firmly stating, 'We'll have to be extremely diligent in monitoring the time we spend demerged. You must understand that on this plain we may have completely different merging characteristics than our previous ones…'

'Yeah, the puking's still a real bitch,' Jank interrupted,

165

hoping his more light-hearted approach would ease the evident strain she was feeling. 'Yet that aside, it'll be a whole lot better now we can share the guard duty openly and yes, leastways till you've fully determined the scope of the security system and whether or not a physical guard is indeed necessary.'

Staring up into his face while the last of the daylight completely vanished, Kat permitted a small smile to make its way to the edge of her mouth. And although Jank's words were what she, herself had been about to say, nonetheless felt obligated to re-enforce it with her own insistent, 'Don't forget we've still to reorganise our own departments and prioritise the smaller of the day-to-day tasks. Till the surveyors complete a broader survey of the land around us, I do insist we keep base camp under soul surveillance.'

'Aye we know, and you'll get no arguments about most of that from us lassie. But ye have ta acknowledge we work well together. Look how grand the meeting room is and, as Jannie grumped, all in less than a week,' Mac assured her.

'Yes, it is,' Annabella hurriedly interrupted. 'Sorry, I meant to ask earlier but we kept getting side-tracked with something else. Do you know if you really need to remerge and what's it feel like if you've been apart too long, and…'

'Oh okay, sorry myself Anne,' Jank broke in with a frowning apology. 'I thought we'd covered this. Like Kat's merge, my lot found we could quite comfortably live apart so long as we have regular physical contact with our three counterparts.'

'Aye laddie and ye also told us each plain mayhap be different dinna ye? So 'tis really up to the God's inna it.'

'One God Mac, only the First to Be and Creator of All really owns that particular title,' Kat softly chastised. 'But come on, if we're going to get into all this again, I need a soft chair and a cold beer.'

A fiery burst of sparks shot into the cool evening air when William added more kindling to the newly lit fire, its budding warmth a welcome deterrent to the rapidly dropping temperature as Kat sat down beside him and tried to sort out a less complicated way to answer the remainder of Annabella's questions.

'When we're apart too long we become very lethargic and cognitive reasoning tends to go out the window. In our experience you have about half a day to re-merge or else piling anomaly onto anomaly, you instantly begin to revisit any less-savoury habits your merge mates or you yourself might have... Which as I'm sure you would understand, could be a tad embarrassing.'

'That aside, a merge in itself will at times be pretty debilitating. Add a late one and you end up feeling like crap. We may not be able to die any more, but it sure doesn't stop you wanting too,' Jank warned. 'Thankfully it's only happened to us on the odd rare occasion. Unfortunately, they were all extra-long callouts which sent everything into the crappy and crappier realm. Thus, you should listen to what your body tells you all the time.'

'So, we canna die although we can be harmed. We can merge and unmerge.'

'Demerge,' Jank amended.

'Aye demerge. Ye can feel sickish and feel wee pains,' Mac frowned, brandishing both his fists in Jank's direction. 'We can attest to that wee fact canna we not laddie?'

'Blood oath.'

Sprawled in the chair separating the two men. Buster was

167

quick to contradict the pair when he declared, 'Actually that might not be true for everyone. Wawura didn't feel any real pain at all when she broke her leg. She merely felt the mending stiffness of the consequences.'

Her dislike of the nick-name he'd used saw Janelle levitate a pile of twigs then hurl the mass at the Master Archivist with a flourish of a neatly manicured finger.

Lobbing her own projectile through the fire's leaping flames towards William, Michaela laughed as it fell at his feet, 'Me too, I've never felt anything more than a few aches and bruises since one of my earliest returns from the physical plains and neither has Will.'

'Never?' A surprised Annabella asked. 'Not even a slightly bad headache?'

'No, not really. Guess we're lucky that way,' Michaela shrugged.

'Conversely, we do suffer from the disadvantages of the injuries we incur and now motion sickness appears to be in play. Thus, as Bustie is wont to say, it's not all booze and bonzer Sheila's,' William added.

'Okay, now I'm really confused,' Annabella groaned. 'If you only feel a bit more than a few tiny pains and aching muscles, how do you know if you're really damaged?'

'Er... Most things don't work that well when they're injured sweetie. My leg doesn't hurt nevertheless it won't support itself and, unless I want to risk doing some seriously bad damage to it, for now anyways I need the crutch and moon boot,' Jannelle explained, swinging the former about in the air before utilizing the momentum she'd built up to hit the back of Buster's head as hard as she could.

'See... No pain,' she grinned. 'Yet betcha, if you feel this

168

over-grown brat's head, you'll find a bump the size of a chook egg sprouting out of it.'

'Oow he has too,' Annabella cried, leaning around Jank to run her hand across the rapidly growing lump on the immense man's head. 'But you can feel my hand?'

'Yeah, I can feel everything from the faintest breath of wind on my cheek to a clout on the head from yon bully,' Buster laughed. 'It just doesn't hurt that much, if at all.'

'Thhuuus you feel pleasure but not necessary pain,' Mac snickered.

Carefully tossing the diminutive golden casket his father had given him from one elegant hand to the other, Bro sat cross-legged in the bough of his second favourite gum tree. Head tilted to one side, and with Sophia once again curled up in his lap bathing her triangular ears, he listened intently while the companions ran through the events of the day.

But when a small Night Jar hooted a soft good morning as it flew past on silent wings he told Sophia, *Time for the troops to get to bed else they won't be fit for anything tomorrow...*

ON PLAIN: DAWN THE NEXT DAY

Allowing the dredges of her night's slumber to meander away before sitting up. Michaela chuckled as she looked down at her still slumbering mate. Her fingers tapping out a muffled tattoo on the doona cover when the memory of her last waking moment surfaced and she sent out a fond, *Got us again, dear Master? Well, good morn to thou beloved and thanks for the excellent sleep.*

The warmth of his distant, *Good morn yourself, little one,* brightening her mind as only he could.

'Sexy if you're going to chat to yourself can you please not do the hand actions?' William burbled a few seconds later, flipping onto his back to peer bleary eyed up at his soulmate. 'I'm getting seasick.'

With a quick goodbye sent to Bro, Michaela planted a kiss on William's mouth then murmured against his lips, 'Sorry just saying good morning to the Boss.'

'What happened to goodnight... Him too?'

'Who else would be game enough to put the plains Ambassadors to bed?'

'Let's see, there's the kids and Mac and...'

'Okay, so that's should've been has the ability to put us to bed. He didn't exactly own up to it, but I'll bet my morning cappa it was the Master.'

'If yesterday is anything to go by it could also apply to several of our mates.' But refusing to debate anything more until he'd had his breakfast and first cup of coffee William pulled himself into a sitting position and added an amused, 'Mmm the nighties not exactly sexy... But the cockatiels are cute.'

'Always are. Look, this one's wearing diapers.'

'Personalized night wear. You have to admire Bro's sense of humour if not his tactics,' William said, running a finger over her flannelette nightgown and across the raised motif of a cockatiel and hermit crab, both of whom were curled up in bed reading a book.

With a wistful sigh Michaela pointed to his own pyjama top, which was dotted with tubby wombats who wore purple waders and had a fishing rod thrown over one shoulder while a white Goshawk roosted on the other, before gently kissing the pewter droplet of her necklet.

'Yeah, he's got our little rascals down pat, hasn't he? I do miss them... And are you by any chance planning on going fishing sometime soon?'

'As do the rest of us Mentors, and I haven't been fishing since we got here.'

'No yet by the looks of things you're planning too, aren't you my darling, Mr Surveyor?' Michaela laughed, then shaking her head at his protests of innocence she threw back the bedcovers and began to shed her nightwear as she walked towards the bathroom.

Loath to sleep alone, it had taken all of the Jank's verbal expertise to convince Alb he'd be perfectly capable of standing the last four-hour shift with his merge mates. Nevertheless, as they stood beside the track at the northern end of the waterhole, he was glad it was over.

171

'Once Kats up,' he said, turning to address his sibling. 'Amber and I will be hitting the sack, okay?'

'Yeah, cheers Jank. Killy wants to catch up with Mum then we'll probably follow you,' Nimble yawned. 'It's been few centuries since Boot Camp.'

'At least, we've had more than our hour of exercise,' Amber dryly muttered.

Smiling up at his wife and thinking how lovely she looked as the early morning sunshine formed a halo out of her golden ringlets Jank rubbed his cramping calf muscle as he winced, 'And some I'd have thought.'

'Is that okay Kil?' Amber asked.

'No probs.' Without commenting on the sudden rosiness of Amber's cheeks. Killy opened the pale blue circle centred in the middle of her communication bracelet then its viewing screen with two nods of her head. 'The merge mates are standing four-hour shifts. Leaving the others free to organise the rosters.'

'Will and Bust have almost finished the surveying and no doubt Mac will find a way to wheedle his way into going again,' Amber laughed.

Maybe we can too, Nimble thought winking at Jank. *I haven't been fishing in ages.*

Relishing the telepathic bond which had begun to flourish between them over the past twenty-four hours the two women playfully admonished in unison, *We heard that one… You go, we go.*

There was a lively discussion going on around him when Gohal turned from watching a small family of Bennet wallabies nibble at the undergrowth. The last dregs of his

172

morning coffee quickly swallowed as he checked the time and just as hastily stood up. Dressed for his day's workload in dark green cargo pants, body shirt and with feet shod in sturdy work boots. His quietly confident voice echoed around the tree wrapped hollow as an expectant quiet settled over the breakfast tables.

'Good morning to those I haven't yet spoken to. I'm Gohal, Mac's Team Leader and he's given me the dubious honour of sitting in on today's rostering meeting. Apparently, our illustrious clan Chieftain… Sorry, that's Training Collator, has duties elsewhere.'

'Going fishing are you, Mac?'

'Nay… Not at all,' the indignantly Scot said, swivelling his head to frown at the five newcomers sitting behind him. 'Ye understand we have ta finish our exploration of this little bit of heaven we've landed on, dinna ye?'

It took the loud rattle of a teaspoon against the inside of Gohal's metal mug to stop the derisive hoots which answered Mac's growled reply from getting out of hand.

Firmly keeping his own dubious opinions to himself. He defended Mac with a laughing, 'Indeed you do,' before adding a more business like, 'Therefore the surveyors are departing at seven thirty. Merge mates when not on parameter duty or rest break please report to T. Thomas at the building site… Stand up and introduce yourself again cobber.'

Nervously ducking his head prior to giving the group a one fingered salute. T. Thomas drawled a quiet, 'Morning all,' then sat down at a far faster sped than he'd used to rise.

'The rest of us will be working on the rostering systems.'

'The merge fronts need some time today to go over a few things,' Annabella reminded the sandy haired man.

173

'Aye sweet lady we do,' Mac said as he winked across the table at the svelte beauty. 'But not until we're home this evening, I'm afraid.'

The chagrin washing over her friend's face made Michaela proclaim with sugary sweetness, 'Anybody who's supposed to be at the meeting and isn't... Shall just have to abide by our decisions, won't they?'

'Fairness is a primary element, so remember honour dictates you play fair ladies,' William warned, giving his soulmate's long plait a firm tug as her expression changed to a brazenly devious one.

With so much to do, the rostering committee had stopped for only a brief respite at noon. Although this wasn't a practise they would permit to be implemented in the future, all felt the urgency to have this particular chore completed. But as she saw the numbers on her watch silently click over to sixteen thirty hours, Jannelle absentmindedly took a sip from her cup. Grimacing at the taste of the cold tea she removed the half empty cup with a blunt, *Rack off.*

As her private jest freed her mind to wander from the computer sitting in front of her, the Chief Justice finally thought to ask, 'I suppose the guy's got off all right?'

'Er bit late for that one but yes, honestly you should have seen 'em,' Michaela snickered. 'Burke and Wills couldn't have taken more stuff if they tried and they were going for months not a mere day.'

'Better safe than sorry,' Kat mildly stated.

'Give me a break kiddo. Why did they need fishing rods and the carton of stubbies Mac tried to hide under the tarp? Answer that one, preferably with a straight face if you can.'

Giggling at the silly expression the tiny woman then pulled Annabella said, 'They used a floating trailer for their gear so why not float chairs instead of feet?'

'Methinks they didn't think of it,' Jannelle laughed. 'Pity that.'

The fact that he was well out-numbered by the group of women didn't stop Gohal from banging a hand against the side of his chair. But since he couldn't refute their glib facts yet knew, as did they, that the surveying was a top priority he growled in defence of the three men's actions, 'It has to be done same as this. You know a proper survey can't be done from a float chair which is why Jan didn't go.'

'Nah I don't think I did and even if that's true. Here they could've thought up whatever equipment they required when they required it. Thus, methinks all the stuff they packed wasn't really necessary,' Michaela said, swallowing the rest of her mirth to add, 'Back at it then?'

'No, dammit Michaela. We're a Training Plain so any practise is good practice…Which damn well includes whatever equipment is needed to complete a legal survey when on any physical plain.'

'True sorry,' Michaela said as she brought the palms of her hands together then dipped her head towards Gohal's reddened face.

'So, twenty hours per week by twenty-four people. You sure that'll do it for you, Anne?'

Firmly entrenched in her mind for quite some time, the official breakdown of her portfolio had been thoroughly combed through in the first hours of their meeting. Therefore the Chief Justice's doubling of her staffing levels took Annabella a bit by surprise.

'Err no, I managed to halve that figure Jan. But if you're feeling that generous, I'll take it this time,' the grinning Administrator blithely quipped. 'I'll happily re-adjust the matrix if necessary once we've worked it a few times. Flexibility is the name of the game.'

Annabella had ended the session not long after her tongue in cheek reply. Still another half-hour sped by before the group finally stirred from the table. The short walk from their seats and down the veranda's sandstone steps into the late afternoon sunshine removing enough of the stiffness from her lithe body for Kat to think, *Train,* then grin as she turned and asked, 'Ride anyone?'

'You beaut,' Michaela whooped, eying the engine and the five wooden carriages Kat had materialised with pleasure. 'Reckon we should?'

'No but you will any way,' Gohal said with a wishful sigh, jerking his head towards the building site. 'Count me out. Tom thinks there's a couple of mistakes in the plans for the grey-water distribution plant, therefore I'll see you later.'

Absentmindedly murmuring her farewells, Jannelle stepped forward to touch the orange woollen lining of the nearest carriage before asking Kat if she could drive.

'I'm ready to test this out a bit. Sure you're up for it?'

'Jeez, as I keep telling everyone Kat, I'm fine… But if you want to make yourself useful you could pop this somewhere for me. For some reason the wretched thing chucks a fit and changes its length if I simply magic it away.'

Tucking that titbit of information into her 'ponder over a glass of wine preferably with her feet up' cupboard. Kat decided it would probably suit her purpose better if someone else did drive.

With the temperamental crutch Jannelle had passed over neatly stowed away in the narrow locker behind the front bench, and her companion's harnesses all checked. Kat de-materialized the fifth carriage then asked the Chief Justice to take them up.

'Up?' Jannelle echoed. 'How far?'

'Up, up and away Jan,' Kat sang over the click of her own harness slotting into place. 'Take us up, up and away.'

'Hang on a sec,' Annabella said as she turned to give the central fastener of the petite blonde's seat-belt a good tug. 'If you only want to see what's around why don't we just, you know, circle up and fly?'

'Because you need to practice first,' Michaela frowned, sticking her elbow up to show Annabella the large purple bruise she now sported. 'It's not as easy as it looks. Personally, I'd much rather stick to float transport.'

'Small steps Anne and safety first. One broken leg is enough. You can experiment all you like once the training mats are finished,' Kat reminded her. 'Above the tree-tops, please Jan, then head east.'

At the top of the tall belt of trees which divided the Billabong from the paddock they'd built the meeting room on Annabella chirped in amazement, 'Oh my goodness, it really is magic this home of ours... Look there's the camp.'

Skilfully avoiding the tips of a red blossomed gum tree. Jannelle slowly steered them over the crowd of busting activity going on around the tents and primary building site.

For crying out bloody loud... First week on a new bloody plain and nobody's worried about strange aircraft? Kat cursed when only waving hands and upturned faces grinned at them as the train's shadow passed over the people below.

177

Curtly ordering her communication bracelet to activate its notebook feature. The young Chief of Security began to verbalize what she suspected would be quite a long list.

'Straight ahead is south Jan,' she said as her narrowing eyes analysed the terrain they were heading towards. 'Crank it up a couple of gears. Let's see how long it takes to reach the foothills. Michaela the left side please, Annabella the right. We want further info on water, land and natural defences.'

A scant fifteen minutes later saw the four idling high above the wide span of fertile grazing land of the eastern paddock.

'Well, that was fun,' Jannelle laughed over her shoulder at the trio behind her. 'Anyone for up for some more loop de loops?'

Pushing long, blue tipped, fingers through her wind-swept hair Annabella said, 'I'm game. How fast was our quickest lap?'

'We just clocked one fifty k's or there about. So, it was pretty flaming fast mate,' Jannelle happily bragged.

Entrenched in the beauty of the western snow-capped tiers, the highest of the mountain range which appeared to almost encircle their new home, it took Michaela several moments to realise what she'd thought had been a darker spot of rock was actually moving towards them.

'Farks,' she yelled. 'Something's coming our way. Nine o'clock and it's no flopping bird or else we're sharing a plain with a flock of flying Bullock-ornis planei.'

Throwing a bewildered look towards where Michaela had indicated Jannelle questioned, 'A what?'

'Body armour and weapons everyone,' Kat spat out. 'And it's a bloody great carnivorous duck.'

Now armed and relatively calmly watching the dot grow larger by the second Michaela laughed, 'That's one way to describe it.'

'Umm it's only the guys,' a rather sheepish feeling Annabella said, her accelerated heart rate automatically slowing when she'd looked through her binoculars and caught sight of Mac's fiery red hair.

'Dammit to hell so it is.' Lowering her own pair of eyeglasses Michaela turned around as she asked, 'What the blazes are they doing up here?'

'Let's go find out, shall we?' Kat snarled. 'Jannelle put the sun to our backs.'

Lined up next to each other Buster flashed the women one of his brilliant grins. Oblivious to the red spots of anger on Kat's otherwise wan face the immense man cried a welcoming, 'Hi there, ladies. Worked out our little surprise, did you?'

'Ye ken it sure beats hoofing it, dinna it,' a surprisingly more astute Mac slowly added as William reached over to pat Michaela's hand and whispered, 'Having fun yet?'

Brushing his hand away to caress the wooden stock of the sawn-off shotgun cradled in her arms a scathing Michaela retorted, 'It's not a bloody surprise and no, you scared the bejeezers out of us you idiots… I nearly punched holes in the lot of you.'

'And bloody well should have,' Jannelle cried, the aftershock of the fright they'd momentarily had making her voice rise with every word.

'Ye nay can kill us, can…'

A no less upset Annabella waved her arsenal of knives under Mac's chin. Slicing off a chunk of his red whiskers she gagged the rest of his sentence by shoving it into his mouth.

'Nooo…' She hissed. 'But we can certainly carve bits off you, you stupid big galoot.'

'I want every one of you fools in the meeting room in five minutes. Jannelle I'm driving.'

With this, Kat took charge of the train and before the men could muster any kind of response, abruptly departed.

'Oh, jolly jumbucks… Now we're in for it,' Buster groaned.

'Aye, methinks Miss Kitty-Kat's a wee bit peeved.'

'Peeved or otherwise, it's all a lot of old cods waddle,' William grunted. 'Come on. We may as well get it sorted now.'

Kat's blunt, 'Thanks everyone I'll see you later.'

Muttered while she leapt from the barely stopped train made it quite clear she didn't wish for any assistance. Thus, having replaced Jannelle's crutch with their weapons of choice the three women dawdled along the sandy track towards base camp.

'Kat's pretty mad, isn't she?'

'Yes… And rightly so don't you think?' Michaela replied, somewhat taken aback by the doubt she heard in the svelte woman's tone.

'Not exactly.' Stopping to turn and stare from one to the other Annabella justified her adjusted support of the supposedly errant trio with a blunt, 'Well they weren't alone, were they?'

'Kat's the Chief of Security. The tenet of our charter clearly dictates this is precisely the sort of stuff they should clear with her first,' Jannelle curtly rebutted.

Annoyed by the cutting crispness of Jannelle's tone, Annabella stiffly retorted, 'Kat's colours are flying high and surely it's only an infringement of the law, if that. Anyways they're not flopping babies and it's not like anyone got hurt.'

'Dammit Annie, my finger was one thought away from blasting the lot of 'em them out of the sky. It could have been disastrous,' Michaela half-heartedly argued. 'Plus, you had more knives than Ned Kelly would've had cold lunches.'

'That's true I sure did... Should've gone for the bow and arrows or maybe a boomerang and spears,' Annabella frowned. 'Knives would've let a real foe get to close.'

Aware her voice had been far sharper than necessary a contrite Jannelle nodded apologetically in Annabella's direction.

'Sorry about that, bloodthirsty lot aren't we... I thought of mounting a Gatling gun in front of me but I wasn't sure about the weight ratio.'

Even though she grinned at the picture Jannelle's words drew. The downward slant of her see-sawing emotions forced Michaela to say, 'Well, we've only been here a week and most of us have been a part of some pretty hairy call outs on the physical plains... No sense going at all if you're bumped back to the Assessment Arches in the first five minutes is there?'

'Unless you're supposed too,' Jannelle mused. 'Anyways it didn't happen and you can be pretty sure Ms Chief of Security will set them straight on a few things.'

'In some ways I almost wish I'd insisted on going with her,' Michaela said with an unpleasant snarl. 'But fun, isn't it? Flying I mean.'

Much happier at this turn of their conversation Annabella smiled down at Michaela. The memory of her last holiday plastering itself to the fore of her mind as she laughed, 'Squillions better than the simulators on the Vacation Plain and

I thought those were pretty cool.'

'I've never even had a go,' Michaela grumbled. 'The blasted things were out of order whenever Will and I visited.'

'Oh, I didn't realise they were linked to the glitch period.'

'Yep, every flopping one… Annnnd our travelling arrangements always seemed to go askew no matter how organised Will made us. Annnnd there's still no sort of reasonable explanation for any of it. All of which makes my man a crabby old…'

'Yeah, we know,' Jannelle giggled before Michaela could get the last of her sentence out. 'I keep forgetting you two have been soul-mated forever.'

'Not forever. Just since we married,' Michaela replied with a fondly wry grin of her own. 'But I must admit… There was the odd, rare occasion it might've felt like an eternity, and that goes for both of us.'

ON PLAIN: BOYS WILL BE BOYS

Her keen hearing picked up the soft tread of rubber on wood yet Kat didn't swing round until the four men came to a halt. The stillness of the hall echoing with the shuffle of feet as they formed a haphazard line behind her ridged body.

'Kat we dinna mean to upset ye wee one.'

It hadn't taken them long, but long enough for Kat's temper to finally par down into equal parts of anger and concern. Marrying together as she judged their expressions, the information gleaned moderated her tone to a derisive, 'Well you have, and were any of you prepared for a hostile attack. Were any of you thinking at all? Were...'

'Your were's are overrated, Kat,' William butted in. 'We saw you rise above the tree-tops.'

'Once we'd walked the paddock that is, doing a complete soil analysis every three metres thus all four quadrants are now finished,' Buster was quick to add. 'We also checked out some animal trails then needed to head home if we wanted to be back by dark... As so ordered.'

'You went past the foothills? You damn fools. Everyone was told the aerial defences stop at the other side of the fields.'

'Which isn't much good iffen we've only got those ta farm,' Mac argued patting his stomach with a large, freckled hand. 'We were famished 'tis hard work this surveying, do ye not know?'

'What the hells that got to do with anything? If you're

183

hungry just bloody well think and if you haven't got anything more informative to say kindly shut up,' Kat snipped before asking Buster if he had anything else to say.

Quailing under the chillness in the look she bestowed on him. Buster found himself stuttering badly as he tried to answer.

'Wwwe um thought wwe'd see, um iifff we could find some more ffffresh wwwater. So wwwe, wwwell. Wwill sssuggested, cccool idea mmmate...'

Sympathy for the huge man and disliking the condescending way Kat had spoken, William coldly admitted, 'I suggested we try to see how far and high the float chairs would take us. And I'd be really surprised if we're the first to do so.'

'Nothings been recorded therefore not prior to today, and as Chief of Security you should've cleared it with me first. That's why we wear the bloody comms bracelets,' Kat shot back with equal coldness.

William bit off the harsh words he wanted to spit out. Staring down at his petite niece for a long moment, he reluctantly acknowledged the honesty of her statement with a curt sideward nod.

'That pocketed,' he shrugged. 'We're the survey team not children Kat. There's a nice little lake behind the first set of foothills. If we hadn't decided to take to the skies it could've, and most probably would've, been weeks or possibly months until we widened our scope enough to find it... Annnnd it will make an excellent second settlement site.'

'Aye the terrain around it is as fertile as our ring of land. There's a good stand of hardwood and plenty of wee fishes in yon lake.'

Flexing her arms to aid the tension of the past ten minutes drain away, Kat looked at each man again before saying, 'All right, scolding done nonetheless in future lodge your intent prior to acting... And you and your bloody fish.'

'Aye lass. Us and our bloody fish. Would ye care ta join me and me wee sweet Irish rose for dinner ta night?' Mac politely queried. His face moulding into a mask of innocent virtuosity which fooled no one, especially not the brown eyed Chief of Security.

'Thanks, and no thanks,' Kat finally laughed. 'Now... From the start. What else did you find?'

Not much later, Michaela stood in front of the large mirror hanging on the canvas wall of her bathroom watching the last strand of her long, dark hair weave itself into an intricate bun at the back of her neck. Giving it a last satisfied pat, she turned around and walked back into the living area of the tent.

'Hi sexy, looking good, babe,' William said.

'Why thank you good sir and so are you,' Michaela replied, thinking the stylish cut of the maroon shirt and snug fitting jeans he'd donned after his shower only added to his stern good looks.

Tweaking a straying corner of the lacy tablecloth into place. The tiny woman glanced at him through a curtain of eyelashes as she murmured, 'The table settings lovely thank you. I wasn't sure you'd have time to do it. Didn't you have er, a meeting with Kat after you came home?'

'Mmm we did.'

'Well?'

'Well, what?'

'What did she say? She was bloody ropable with you

guys,' Michaela admonished. 'And so was I for that matter.'

'Can't say I noticed. Too busy defending myself from a gun toting midget.'

'Reach for the sky partner.'

'Ouch don't, that'll leave a bruise,' William laughed, backing away from the fingernail she jabbed into his ribs as she sat down. 'But seriously, I don't understand what all the fuss was about. We saw you leave... Besides Bust and I would've always known who you were.'

'How?'

'Honey, apart from using my eyes, I'd know your thought pattern anywhere and Bust said Jan's also easy to recognise.'

'Flop it all, we tried that but it didn't work.'

'Maybe it's only something we males are able to do?'

Although her hackles rose, Michaela didn't bother disputing his interpretation of what had or hadn't occurred. Telling him they'd put it down to distance over the peel of the bell attached to the side pole of their tent and Nimble's loud, 'You lot decent?'

It hadn't meant to be more than pre-dinner drinks, William's breakfast issued invitation. Growing as the day aged, his hope for a late dinner alone with his wife had sunk with the orange sunset. The table he'd laid with much anticipation now a bed for a cluster of crumbs and a small pile of empty plates. The rest offered to his guests along with a heavily loaded recommendation that the finger food would taste better eaten in the comfort of their own tents.

'Not yet, you guys have an eternity for the mushy stuff,' Killy teased in reply to the man's most recent request for the last of their visitors to go home. 'My curiosity is starving even if my bellies full, so what's it like up there?'

'Dangerous.'

The two Ambassadors might've hosted the evening. But it had been Buster's highly entertaining yarns about the seedier aspects of his craft that kept the party flowing well past William's clearly stated timeframe. Yet by the lightness of the farewells he'd received, a refreshing happenstance and an ideal way to erase the weariness of the past week from Talaa's budding community.

And the reason why William massaged his soulmate's thin shoulders as he dryly stated, 'Some of the natives are really dangerous.'

Aren't we the founding members? Amber thought while a worried look flickered over her face and she reached for Jank's hand.

'Yep, we sure are. He meant me,' Michaela answered, before muttering a silent, *Oh, crappola,* when William hastily shushed her the same way.

'We're not connected yet you knew what I thought,' Amber softly exclaimed, glancing down at the small gap which divided them then upward again to study the tiny Ambassadress like she would a dragonfly caught under a half circle of glass.

'Evolution, my dear sister-in-law, evolution,' Nimble guessed, his eyes switching from one parent to the other while he added a mildly grumbling, 'Though I'm not too sure I like the idea of you lot willie-nillie reading my mind.'

'I'm sorry... But it's not universal so I can't do it with everyone,' Michaela admitted, both pleased and relieved Amber seemed to find the idea more intriguing than upsetting. 'It's just another thing we need to iron out... Soon too, privacy's everyone's right.'

'Mmm, well as long as it stays out of our personal quarters, I can live with it for the present. Anyways its only partial evolution,' Jank grinned. 'Which clearly needs figuring out or else Mum wouldn't have pointed a loaded shotgun at Dad would she?'

Not needing telepathy to comprehend the cagey expression which darkened Michaela's large, blue eyes Killy said, 'It wasn't armed.'

'Would've been if...'

'Dammit Michaela,' William sharply interrupted. 'Wasn't it even bloody loaded?'

'You guys never change...' Nimble sighed. 'Dad's overprotective and mum's always pushing his buttons.'

'Flapping, flipping, flopping oath I do not. Besides who pressed who's buttons?' Michaela protested, her nose rising as she lifted her head up to peer under half closed eyelids at her youngest child. 'They were the ones that came barrelling out of the sun like a flock of demented...'

This time it was Amber who halted whatever Michaela was about to say when she cut in with another worried, 'It wasn't armed. You just owned up to that particular fact Mickey.'

'We had binoculars... Do you really think I don't recognise Will when I see him? Besides it takes less than a Nano second to load something by brain power. Well, so long as you know what ammo it uses.'

ON PLAIN: OBSERVATION ONLY

The weeks have just flown, Michaela thought, shooing aside the float chair which partially blocked the doorway into the meeting room before walking over to the large blueprint hanging on the side wall.

Though there were a number of cosmetic touches left to finish externally, it was nice to see most of the pre-requisites for the interior of the main complex had been completed. Yet more curious to see how many more nights they'd have to spend sleeping in a tent, she touched the forward icon and skimmed past several more templates before coming to her own quarter's floor plan.

Bobbing out from behind the pile of boxes stacked in front of the small stage attached to the far end of the room. Annabella laughed when Michaela began a spate of irritated swearing.

'Chill Mickey. They've just been a bit slack marking things off, but you've been sent the adjusted updates. If we weren't going out today you would've been in your new abode nearly a fortnight ago. So, blame Bro if you're going to have a hissy fit.'

Thrusting back the sleeves of her rugby top as the svelte woman walked towards her Michaela grumped, 'Look, I'm covered in mozzie bites. The little sods think I'm a bloody pork roast and they itch like billyo.'

'Yeah, but you're old enough not to scratch them sweetie,'

189

Annabella replied, grimacing at the bundle of red edged scabs on her friend's lower arms. 'Haven't you heard of a citronella candle or mayhap insect repellent?'

'Suppose I should have thought of that... How longs it gonna be now then? Because not everyone's going on today's jaunt around the cosmos.'

'Tom reckons we'll be in our own places three days after we come back.' Empathising with the reason behind the despondent set of Michaela's shoulders Annabella gave her hand a friendly shake. 'Come on, cheer up Madame Ambassadress. It's only an Observation trip and like our esteemed Master said, someone has to keep things ticking over here.'

'It's Talaa for crying out loud, any one of us could do that. I haven't even walked to the bottom of the foothills and...' Refocused by the beeping alarm on her armlet and the sound of excited voices that had begun to drift in through the open doorway. Michaela bit down on the rising wave of angry disappointment which had become her constant companion since being confronted by the unbending wall of iron behind Bro's flippant refusal to alter either the names or positions of the personal who would participate in their plain's maiden voyage. Then put as much warmth as she could muster into her ruefully added, 'Sorry, please continue to ignore my whinges, past and present, and make sure you stay safe okay, for methinks the shows about to start. Ready?'

Smiling briefly at Annabella's animated response. The tiny woman rose to slowly climb the stairs to the top of the stage. For although over the past few months everyone had met and worked with their Master in person, thus no other clarification should really be needed, she knew her latest piece of news wouldn't be a welcome one.

'Good morning, as you're well aware the previous four weeks have been used to research and prepare for specific eras,' Michaela said in way of an opening preamble. 'Unfortunately, something must've cropped up elsewhere because Bro's made some minor, his words not mine, adjustments. Which unfortunately means two of our teams are now going to potentially unknown times. Yet onward we go, thus if you wouldn't mind, please follow me… The departure chamber awaits our presence.'

Retracing her earlier steps Michaela strolled over to the far side of the room to press the triangular rune centred in the fifth, of nine, wooden panels. Separating the hall's polished floorboards from its high domed ceiling, these intricately carved works of art covered the entire western wall.

There were no windows to break the plainness of the lilac hued walls of the hexagonal chamber the retracting door unveiled, but nor were they needed. The rectangular skylights used to form the bulk of the conical roof, most depicting the flora and fauna of the Tasmanian bush, allowing ample light to flood the room with rainbows of soft colour.

Five oblong platforms, each with a number of plush armchairs bolted to their bases, edged the perimeter of the chamber. The central dais where Jannelle would stand, it's only other visible piece of equipment.

''Tis a bit different from the wee practice simulators you designed for us laddie.'

'Everything works the same way. They've just been spiffed it up a bit,' Jank assured the tall scot.

Running a hand over the cool material of the closest seat, Michaela called for silence then announced, 'If necessary, your final objectives have already been readjusted and coded into the computer of your environmental craft. Please take your places on the chairs matching the colour of your communications bracelet.'

Not having seen the final product but aware she'd and the Chief Justice had stayed up most of the night 'fussing' as William called it. Jank dropped a quick kiss on top of his mother's head.

'Good stuff, your tastes improved,' he murmured before walking over to sit in the forward seat of his merge's platform.

Lightly tapping the pale blue button imbedded into the middle of the chairs right hand armrest, the Master Technician pursed his lips when the computer flared into life, and he saw their revised destination.

His quiet, 'Change of venue guys,' remaining unclarified as Michaela once again asked for the room to quieten.

'Like you can see we kept it as unencumbered as possible,' she said. 'Press your merge-coloured button for control access. Large mauve one for engaging or disengaging viewing shields. Purple for sub-relay communication, orange for idle, green for go and the portable Archivers went live five minutes ago…Mac, you okay?'

Asked because everyone knew Mac continued to feel unworthy of his position on the plain, Michaela wasn't really surprised when the Scotsman nodded towards the forward seat where Gohal sat with a somewhat defensive, 'Aye… And like ye no doubt have noticed, Goh twill be in tha' driving seat.'

'Mmmaaac,' Jannelle sighed, without looking up from the lectern's instrument panel. 'Thus, I figure if we need to contact you it will be via him?'

The slight censure in the Chief Justice's query made Mac

duck his head, then respond with an upward glance and a scowled, 'Och woman, since we'll be on open band it mayhap be anyone of us.'

What is, is. Leave the man alone Jannie, Buster chided, casting his eyes over each craft one more time before taking his place next to William.

'I'm sorry Mac. Guess you're not the only nervous one. Check communication bracelets everyone.' Receiving the requested canopy of checked and double-checked Jannelle went on to order, 'Engage shields… Three, two, one, activate.'

And while the glass, then metal environmental shields rose to encase the launching pads Michaela linked arms with Jannelle's and whispered a last, 'Au revoir. Safe travels everyone,' as Talaa's first official deployment to the physical plain vanished from the chamber.

ON PLAIN: JUST US

For a moment or so, only their breathing disturbed the heavy silence which fell over the two women when the faint hum the departing crafts discharged also seeped away.

'Now nowt but us.'

'Don't forget Sophie.'

'I said us.' Frowning down at the fluffy kitten curled up at their feet Michaela sighed before murmuring a more cheerful, 'Ahhhh well, whatever... Now what old stick?'

'You're older than me and they've left us enough work for the next ten years,' Jannelle glumly retorted, pointing to the piles of clipboards and USB sticks on the shelf below the instrument board. 'Here, take a gander at this.'

Yet when the overhead clouds wandered away and Jannelle peered upwards. Her woes were momentarily forgotten as she became lost in the pictorial story the skylights told. Gazing from one pane of glass to the next, she found it easy to identify the different species of animals and vegetation Michaela had chosen to illustrate. But lovely as these were, it was the portrait of Bro introducing himself to the merge teams she favoured the most.

'You've captured everyone's likenesses perfectly,' she said in admiration. 'Including your own.'

'Thanks, though I should've used a bit of artistic licence and air brushed out some of the wrinkles around my eyes... But too late now, thus how about a spin around the complex prior to knuckling down?'

'The last time we did that it put us a day behind... I recommend work until lunch, play later.'

'Aww come on a couple of hours wouldn't be too much of a delay,' Michaela wheedled, bending over to lift Sophia on top of her shoulder before picking up a handful of the USB sticks.

But seeing the unconvinced expression the Chief Justice still wore when she passed along the next handful. Michaela grudgingly volunteered to cook lunch and dinner.

'Both meals plus clean up?'

Not prepared to let the woman get the best of her so easily. Michaela remained tight lipped until she'd loaded herself up with the leftovers.

'Both meals,' she finally echoed.

'And clean up.'

'You can help with that or you know, I can always go on my own...'

Loudly dropping the pile of work they'd been left on the desk nearest to the main entrance of the meeting room Michaela growled, 'Well?'

Ignoring the tiny woman's disgruntled mien Jannelle placed an arm around her shoulder and letting her actions speak for themselves, guided her out the door. Michaela's gleeful shout almost deafening Jannelle when they stopped at the edge of the veranda and saw the colourful divan hovering several inches off the ground at the bottom of the steps.

Bro agreed with you cobber... Thus, your chariot awaits. Sweet man.

Eagerly escaping the confines of Jannelle's arm, Michaela

capered down the wide blocks of sandstone. In less than a minute she had herself and the purring feline securely buckled up, and was somewhat impatiently urging her slower moving companion to hurriedly do the same.

With the couch's drive console already engaged. Jannelle quickly ran through the mandatory checklist the Travel Authority insisted be done every time this mode of transport was used. Then embracing the heady feeling of freedom surging through her veins, drove them up into the azure sky.

Perched in the vee of his favourite tree, Bro pushed aside a branch laden with red flowers and fragrant gum leaves. An impish twinkle settling in his eyes when he saw the trio stop to watch a pair of Gosh hawks glide in and out of the cool currents of air that flounced down from the tree dappled foothills.

'Hi ladies, room for one more?'

'Shite, I wish he wouldn't do that,' Michaela complained, her eyes automatically flying towards the dense foliage of the tallest gum tree she could see. 'Eleven o'clock, got him?'

Already having glimpsed the man Jannelle muttered a soft, 'Damn sure,' before directing a much stronger, 'No there isn't, and you damn well shouldn't scare us like that... You'll make us all have heart attacks,' towards their Master.

Bro's deep baritone scuttled back at them as he mumbled a perfunctory 'Sorry,' and a challenging, 'In that case the last one to the training fields is a dilatory dingo.'

The long hours they'd spent honing their mental skills, regardless of the talents draining aftermath, had well prepared the women for just such an occasion. Quick to clasp Michaela's outstretched hand whilst simultaneously weaving her other through Sophia's silky fur, Jannelle teleported them above the training mat. A satisfied smirk lifting the corners of her rosy lips when Bro appeared a second later.

Casually dispersing the small cloud of sweet-smelling mimosa which accompanied him with a flap of his hand. The man leant forward and unclipped the fluffy feline's harness without acknowledging either Michaela's softly hummed, 'We are the champions,' or Jannelle's smug grin.

'Coming aboard ladies…'

But neither woman doubted the violent swinging of their couch, as the grinning man plucked Sophia from her seat before wriggling his lean body into the vacant spot between them, wasn't intentional.

'How about this here field.' Straining his swiftly clipped harness Bro added a forward motion to the divan's sideways tilt when he peered past his sneakered feet at the training mat below. 'You must agree Kat's merge have worked their own magic here.'

Just pleased that their Master's squirming hadn't dislodged the lot of them. Michaela had mixed feelings as she stared downwards to survey the differing heights of the seven flying foxes which criss-crossed the huge quadrangle of navy matting.

'Mmm, and I must confess I do like zipping along those things,' she eventually said.

'Now you mean,' Jannelle teased. 'How many times did you balk at the highest tower?'

'I told you I scared myself witless on one of them on the physical plain…Anything higher than twenty metres gives me the heebee jeebees,' and as a shiver of apprehension ran over Michaela's body she mumbled a pleading, 'No tossing me out of planes when I go operative again please, Boss.'

Careful to shield his, *You'll get used to it little one.*

Bro thought the drinks he'd just handed them away again and with a twirl of his finger, sent them spiralling back up into the cloudless sky.

Mere moments later; though it felt much longer for his human companions, the fearless feline finding it very much to her liking, when the acute ascent came to an abrupt halt several hundreds of meters above the ground, he wisely kept his deep voice to a sympathetic purr as he queried, 'Wanna go play with the hawks?'

Extremely grateful she hadn't had a chance to drink any of the milky coffee he'd given her, Michaela barely managed to shake her head. The rest of her attention remaining fiercely fixated on either regaining her equilibrium or keeping the contents of her stomach in place.

Not so Jannelle, who had no trouble scolding, 'Thanks but no thanks Master...That was really mean. Mickey looks like she's going to barf and my leg's fine now.' Then snickered before adding, 'And I'd prefer to keep it that way.'

'Ooow now that's not nice. I could have been seriously disabled and I'm positive the wall wasn't there before I ran into it.'

'Yeah, and we're damn sure it was,' Jannelle countered without a trace of sympathy for his previous night's misfortune, or the crumpled state of the chair he'd crashed into the southern end of the meeting room. 'So stop whining. It's your own fault, you were just to flipping busy showing off to see it.'

'I don't think it...'

With the aid of a few intermittently swallowed mouthfuls of air Michaela broke in to say, 'Whether it was... Or 'twas not… You… Still would've lost… Oh Clutzy one,' and a more relevant, 'How long can we… Oww… Realistically expect to reside here?'

'I suppose,' Bro slowly granted. 'As to the other, till Dad needs you elsewhere.'

'The last time you conned us with those particular words. I got stuck on the Assessment Plain for like, fifteen bloody decades.'

'Bad analogy. Talaa's nothing like the Assessment Plain,' Jannelle laughed. But her amusement quickly faded, exchanged for an unhappy frown as she tartly added, 'Besides you weren't the only one, I was dumped there too.'

Kissing each woman's cheek, Bro responded with a somewhat annoying, 'Methinks what has been written or seen shall come to pass. Thus, you were re-assigned not conned, stuck or dumped. The timing was merely coincidental with the um, er, other incident and since you all bellyached enough at the time, shall we move on to perhaps a geography lesson instead?'

'Baloney… I'll never believe it was pure chance,' Jannelle refuted, yet for once opted not to take it any further when she added, 'What's on the other side of the mountains?'

'You lot run this place, don't you? Therefore, if you're really keen to know organise a field trip.'

'Who runs what doesn't signify anything. Your memory's definitely getting mushy if you can't recall we actually did the majority of the organisation for this one and as you can see, we're still here,' Michaela rallied enough to tease. 'Oh, we've floated back over the campsite.'

Never having been this high prior to now, Jannelle twisted back and forth while she adjusted her mental picture of the

199

terrain surrounding their new home.

'Circles within circles,' she muttered. 'I don't suppose it escaped your notice the Billabong could be the centre of a large bullseye?'

'Nooo but I doubt it is… Clever, isn't it?

'Not if we're attacked it's not.'

'As if. There's nay poverty, hunger nor wars aloft silly,' Michaela softly chuckled.

'Oh, for Pete's sake, we didn't have much nausea either… So who knows, mayhap somethings gone skewwhiff and everything's now in reverse.'

Rubbing the top of Jannelle's short, windblown hair Bro planted another kiss on her cheek before momentarily stilling.

'Ah see, just like I said. Dad reckons we're doing all right and the settlement is exactly where it should be. Try arguing with that.'

It was their Master's indisputable statement not the satisfied grin he bestowed on the pair. Which saw their conversation turn towards the ins and outs of their next field trip while the divan meandered around the eco-friendly, quite diverse building sites. The morning dribbling its way into the noon time hours as the cloud diminished sunlight found them once more idling high above the safety mat.

'Last one downs a kooky kookaburra,' Bro cried, disengaging their harnesses as he threw his arms over his head and executed a perfect swan dive out of the couch.

'Yuck, he's an idi…' Michaela began, only to halt the rest of her sentence when a feeling of utter horror changed it to a screaming, 'Oh, lord, look ooouuut.'

The extra weight of their bodies hitting the mat mere seconds after their Master sent Michaela on a series of uncontrolled bouncing. Forgetting what she'd been taught about landing on the safety mats till she'd finally stopped moving. She carefully flipped onto her back in time for Sophia's billowing parachute to cover the end of her nose.

Refusing to let Bro to see how terrified she'd been. Michaela didn't say anything as she watched his head swing from an equally quiet Jannelle to herself, then back and forth again from the corner of her eye. Not hurrying as she untangled the unfussed puss, and to keep her burgeoning temper from erupting, the tiny woman set her mind to contextualising the multitude of questions their Master had still to give a straightforward answer to.

Yet obviously bored of counting aloud the variety of expressions which had apparently rolled across their faces. The grinning man attempted to sever the pair's nonresponsive attitude.

'It's been a beaut day so why the frowns ladies?' Sighing when he received neither mental nor verbal response from the two, Bro drawled a firmer, 'As I just asked, why the frowns ladies?'

'Don't bother, for you'll just be wasting good oxygen,' a very controlled Jannelle replied, which was all she was prepared to say about their Master's recent shenanigans.

'Well apart from wanting to vomit again.' Hissing the words without even realising it. As Jannelle leant forward and tapped a warning finger on her knee Michaela added a more restrained but quite sharp, 'Questions just heaps of confounded questions. You don't answer most of our issues or if you do, you give us tonnes more to deal with.'

'I do too, and no I don't.'

'You damn well don't and, yes you do.'

'Do not.'

'Do so and… Annnd everyone's getting heartily sick of it.'

The storm smouldering in Michaela's deep blue eyes squared off against the thunder clouds gathering momentum in Bro's grey ones as their responses spiralled down to a singular word each.

Tempted to leave them to it to see if it would develop into another of their long-winded sparring matches, Jannelle listened for a few more seconds before looking around for a distraction of some kind.

Her startled, 'Gosh where did you come from little one?' Loud enough to suspend the sound of the pair's rapidly accelerating voices.

Dragging his eyes from Michaela's, Bro burst into laughter as he picked up the squirming bundle of fur Jannelle had referred too.

'Hi Em… Girls meet Esmeralda Magic, or as she likes her friends to call her, Em, another of Sophie's merge mates,' he said in way of introduction, then with one of his most beguiling smiles passed the ball of brindle coloured fur to Michaela.

Holding the excited pup in front of her nose, Michaela cooed a welcome while she studied their newest arrival.

Both of the puppy's floppy ears sported a ribbon tied into a thin green bow. Her curious, button brown eyes shining out from beneath shaggy white brows as she returned Michaela's gaze with similar curiosity.

Finding her sense of humour restored and her belly calmed as soon as she'd touched the cute little pup Michaela giggled, 'Excellent, one down, one to go… Pity Mac wouldn't take our bet.'

The gentle touch of Esmeralda Magic's pink tongue licking her outstretched fingers had the same instant effect on Jannelle as it had on the Ambassadress, so she replied to Bro's enquiring look with an amused, 'We thought Sophie might eventually demerge into four like the soul fronts do, and everyone reckoned it'd be a puppy except Mac. He expected a roo.'

'Methinks she may... Methinks she may not,' Bro absentmindedly purred, giving the little Staghound, whose large paws suggested she would one day grow into an exceedingly big animal, a friendly pat. 'Do you like her name? You know how important the letters of a name or the name itself are, and how difficult some are about them.'

'Most aren't as pedantic as a certain person I could mention,' Michaela said with a pointed stare. But having sat through endless lectures pertaining to the meanings of the said things, and since this time it was her who'd given him an excuse for yet another, she quickly murmured a sweetly coy, 'Bro you love us, don't you?'

Screwing his lips to one side to show Michaela he was awake to her blatant digression Bro chanted a loud, 'Group hug... Group hug.'

Eyes closing as she readily complied, Jannelle felt the warmth of her friend's arms envelope her. And when she opened them once more, wasn't in the least surprised to find all trace of daylight gone, traded for the mellow light of a full moon and the huge pile of linen ware which now surrounded them.

'Ah, nights upon us. So, guess it's probably time to see how the troop's days gone. Then we'll play a game, okay?' Bro

203

suggested, dropping his arms to check the numerals embedded into the side of his communication bracelet before lifting Sophia onto his lap.

'Hang on a sec,' Michaela frowned, tapping his velvet clothed knee with one long nailed finger. 'Why on earth do you really need a communication bracelet?'

'You don't know how, you don't go now.'

A touch of frost had entered Jannelle's voice when she stated, 'Wouldn't think that particular motto applies to you... In fact, we know it doesn't.'

The sudden rush of heat that ran up Bro's neck to redden his face caused him to squirm uncomfortably. Hoping it was too dark for either of the women to see the embarrassment it announced he lowered his chin to his chest. Adding momentum to the long strands of blue-black hair that swung forward to curtain off most of his face.

'They never had these or anything like them when I had a physical body and I like gadgets...Who knows, it's possible Dad will send me back.'

'You still wouldn't need mechanical comms, and I thought you're going back was always foreseen.'

'It might've been Jannie... But can you imagine how grand things would've been if I'd never had to go in the first place,' Bro said with a self-bracing sigh. 'Come on link up.'

Designated a daily practice, it was as easy as it had been to breath for Bro to channel their combined power into the communication facet of his silver armlet then think, *Will, Buster report please.*

Replying well within the anticipated time frame it was the Master Archivist they heard cheerfully burble, *Hiya Boss, ladies. Everything's cool. We've just been talking to Kat and*

Annie, and they aren't having any problems. In fact, Kat's team must be having a blast 'cause they seemed, um well, very um happy. Oh yeah, and the other lot checked in earlier on too, and all's hunky dory even if they are a bit wet. Anyways a few drops of water won't hurt 'em. We're pretty waterproof.

Wondering if her soulmate was in the same merry state Michaela asked, *Will my love, anything up the putt with you?*

No, I'm not affected at all, William chuckled. *Unfortunately, Bust continues to feel the emotions and sensations that came through from Kat's team and it seems they've attended a party or two or mayhap even three.*

Already? And dammit, Jannelle swore. *Jank won't be happy. He was sure he'd managed to train that particular idiosyncrasy out of us and yes before you ask, we can only hear you two. Thus, I bow to Bust's insistence on manning a sub-plain relay station and, as to that, any more clues to where in the universe you're squatting?*

Sorry you're starting to crackle again, catch you tomorrow, William said leaving Jannelle's query, like their Master did when later asked, unanswered.

The trio's, *Well stay safe, Au Revoir,* the final words the off plainers would hear before the chain of thought unravelled.

'Having fun aren't they…' Jannelle moaned as she unlinked her hands then sagged back against the pile of plump cushions scattered behind her. 'Happy as two pigs in flaming muck.'

'Yep, sure seem to be.'

'Sure, you don't want us to go help them… Bust really isn't himself you know.'

'Nope, thanks Miss Jan. Dad's Helpers are most likely keeping an eye on them and a bit of fun on an obs assignment isn't against the rules,' Bro refuted, grabbing a spare cushion and tossing it towards the inwardly looking Ambassadress. 'Don't worry Shmich, they're fine.'

'Haven't called me that in a long time Boss,' Michaela softly murmured as she automatically caught and returned the satin encased pillow in one fluid motion. 'But if your dad and his mates are okay with things, who's a mere mortal soul like me to argue?'

'Most of them were alive once too you know, and who I am never stops you from grumping at me.'

'Some say familiarity breeds contempt… Oh Adored one,' Jannelle quoted. 'Couldn't we just go take a quick look? You could work your magic thus we'd be back before we even left.'

'Nope,' Bro repeated. 'No one required babysitting on other trips so why should they on this one. Now twenty questions…'

Twenty questions… More like a bloody thousand, Michaela winced as she broke in with a quickly exclaimed, 'Mac hasn't done this before.'

'For Pete's sake one of his cohorts probably has and even if not, Goh, Mharri and Julz are more than capable of taking a few notes. Thus, desist with thou caterwauling and mind your language… Twenty questions. Mickey, you first.'

Ineffective though it probably was against the man's awesome abilities. Michaela slammed her mind-shield shut while pushing and pulling at the cushions till the safety mat began to wobble like a half set flummery. Utilizing the time spent to prioritise the vagrant reflections that surfed her turbulent brainwaves, the tiny woman then let loose a surfeit of quizzing.

'How many people slash animals can Sophie merge into

annnd why don't the Mentors merge, and what's the number of native species that live here annnd, even if we're the first, are we really the only settlement on Talaa?'

'Without mentioning how rotten your syntax was,' Bro balefully drawled. 'That was a heck of a lot of ands, plus four questions you rattled off.'

When she found herself too blank minded to summon up any kind of dissembling rebuttal, Michaela glared back at him while Jannelle prodded his arm and told him to please just damn well answer something.

Not willing to push their combined displeasure any further, Bro eased the sleepy canine out from under Michaela's arm and carefully stood her in the middle of the triangular space their crossed legs edged.

The ancient kerosene lantern which suddenly appeared a few inches above their Master's head coated the area around them with a candescent glow as he softly whispered, 'Sweet Em, how about you live up to your name…'

Scrambling up from the warmth between Jannelle's jean clad thighs Sophia padded over to rub noses with the long-haired pup. The puss's high-pitched screech the briefest of warnings before she began to shimmer and shake, and two more diminutive creatures flowed from her trembling body.

'Oh… My… Stars… That's brilliant. Like Bust would say, to state the bleeding obvious, Sophie does indeed de-merge into four,' Jannelle laughed, then leant forward to pick up the closest of the newcomers.

The petite foal was a perfect miniature of the black Clydesdale who'd vanished as Sophia reappeared their first night on Talaa. While the fourth of the tiny animals, the previously seen yet to be named Emu chick's head bobbed

207

along with his shyly chirped hello.

'See, I *do* too, answer your questions, Shmich,' Bro tauntingly stressed.

'Sophie and Em gave us the only reply we received and will you please knock off the Shmich stuff.'

The peculiar face Michaela pulled saw Jannelle say, 'Uh uh, no way not until you explain what it signifies. Give, girlfriend, give.'

'She'll tell you later,' Bro grinned, dodging sideways to avoid the closed fist Michaela aimed at his muscled bi-cep. 'Now that's four questions gone for shortie here.'

'One sentence it was only…'

Out pacing whatever further argument Michaela might've rebounded with Bro offered to keep score while producing a long-feathered quill, crystal ink pot and piece of paper.

'You don't need those things. That's what your flopping computers for.'

'Aahh bet he can't,' Jannelle said. 'Because although the dear man likes gadgets doesn't mean he knows how to use 'em.'

'I do so, I just prefer parchment and ink,' Bro huffed, disregarding Jannelle's snort of mockery to protest, 'Stop ganging up on me and get on with it, times a wasting.'

'How about we forget the game because if you'd kindly tell us what you know. I'm relatively certain we'll be able to handle it from there,' Michaela slyly suggested along with a silently thrust, *Shut up Jannie or we'll be here to sunup.*

Inwardly smiling when the two women began to trade insults. Bro cut short their friendly quarrelling with a laughing, 'Sophie wasn't supposed to come with the office furniture you conjured up Shmich. But since Miss Smarty hitched her own ride here, I couldn't really send her back now, could I?'

'Why wouldn't or shouldn't she come? Soph's always moved about with Mickey and Will.'

'However, she wasn't meant to come leastways not now. A cat's instincts are bad for the birds and smaller animals, so too dogs,' Bro frowned. 'Dad kind of wanted this plain to be natural flora and fauna without any new emigrants for a little bit. But since Miss Puss's gang took it upon themselves to tag along, we decided to see what developed. Then by the way they helped you in the war to end all wars...'

His morosely tacked on, 'Well it was supposed to be,' nearly missed as Jannelle spat an acid, 'Which one was that?'

Yeah, and you, yourself, suffered a heinous flaming death for them dearest. And to this very moment, millions still die in the human's senseless frigging wars. At least when my kind kill it's rarely for anything more than bloody sustenance.

Empathizing with her Master's mournful discontentment at how often the Earth's dominant species reverted to warfare instead of his Father's teachings to solve their differences. Sophia rubbed a sympathetic paw across Bro's knee as she finished her silent condemnation with a blast of foully put cursing, then exploited the full range of her vocal cords for another ear-piercing screech when she saw Michaela's mouth begin to open.

'That's just admitting you winged it.' Taken aback by the sudden disheartened slump of Bro's shoulders and the puss's, though quieter, ongoing reaction. A somewhat sheepish Michaela said, 'Oh I'm sorry beloved but you should've known Soph would find a way to be with us. She's awfully smart.'

The ageless feline thanked Bro for the box of chocolate

209

mice he said would be in the fridge when she next visited his quarters before dryly sighing, *Aww bugger it, no matter what Master. They're my family. So they go, I go.*

In an attempt to dispel the gloomy notions swirling around them Bro replied to both when he said, 'Aye but that wasn't the plan, therefore nay everything 'tis written on a magic tablet.'

Charmed by the spell woven through his hopelessly conveyed accent Sophia began to purr while the women chorused an unpractised, 'The guts of it bloody well are, though I prefer murder as opposed to kill.'

'Mmm, I guess kill's hard for some if taken literally, yet seriously ladies taper thou language for I was only joshing... Thus, since there's no point worrying about Ms Sophie's gang now they're here and ignoring anything gloomier. I've told you the native animals on Talaa are, or would've been, found on its physical plain counterpart around the time Buster's ancestors arrived. That'll help, won't it?'

'You did?' Jannelle frowned. 'And if so, you're almost saying we could end up with a plain full of humongous great dinosaur souls.'

'Not likely,' Michaela grinned. 'Considering they died out well before humanity evolved.'

With a dismissive shake of her head Jannelle grunted, 'Oooh put a sock in it, smart aleck. You know what I meant.'

'You don't need domestic animals because you can just think up your food... So, what are you going to do with everybody after you've been here a few centuries?' Bro laughed, wiggling a finger in front of the woman's nose.

Jannelle pushed the neatly manicured digit to one side as she retorted, 'Apart from beginning another plain... It all depends on how much land we've got. Most of the First to Be's creature's soulmate here if not prior to coming aloft and usually offer to adopt at least one embryo as well as have biological kids. Well, if they hadn't already that is.'

'Mother Nature provides plenty of alternative ideas for contraceptives, like how the roos self-manage their breeding in a drought. Maybe we can learn to teach everybody that,' Michaela said, her normally smooth brow wrinkling as she contemplated the difficulties this would undoubtedly incur.

'You know, next he'll be telling us everyone's gunna turn vegetarian,' Jannelle joked.

Without a trace of humour in his voice and frowning at Sophia's indignant, *I like meat.*

Bro puffed up his cheeks then waited till they'd deflated to demand, 'So? What's wrong with that?'

'You're having us on, aren't you? I thought all the animals needed their normally consumed type of food to nourish their souls same as us,' Michaela vigorously contested. 'There might not be enough land suitable to feed even a small populace if we're all vegetarians, and good luck making everybody give up their steaks.'

'Alas therefore, you're probably going to be very busy coming up with a new micro gardening modus operandi... While Chiefie here will be equally as busy trying to format an agreement which appeases all of Dad's creatures and their dietary requirements. Can't have them eating each other, 'cause that wouldn't be polite, would it?' Momentarily freezing, the man's infuriating grin relaxed to spread across his face before he chuckled, 'Sorry, really would love to stay and chat some more however Papa's a calling. Au revoir and tootle pip my sweets.'

211

Gathering the baby animals against her body when Bro's abrupt departure made the mat oscillate again, Michaela dismissed the lantern with a flick of her slender hand.

'Every bloody time... Every bloody time.'

'Yeeeep, every bloody time. Ask one itty bitty little question and he gives us a few hundred more to solve.'

'Herbivore's all of us? That's so... Sooo not how it works elsewhere aloft, and do you reckon the merges will separate any further?'

Jannelle's rhetorical, 'Bro's right you never ask only one,' was pursued by a quick, 'No one here would mind leading instead of following thus it's a possibility. And please shelve the merge bit until their back and ask them in person instead of having us speculate about it till our brains turn to goop like you usually do. Methinks it's about time we fed the littlies and sorted out their sleeping quarters. My bed beckons.'

Then, rolling off the mat with enviable grace, the Chief Justice wagged her outstretched fingers.

'Hand me the babies please mate.'

'One puppy, one kitten, one foal plus note, one emu chick also with envelope,' Michaela counted.

With the note that had been newly tied to the foal's collar read and popped away in a trouser pocket Jannelle squatted on her haunches in front of the four tiny animals.

Kissing the diminutive horse on his nose and being soundly licked in return she laughed, 'Welcome to your new home Imco. I'm Jannelle and she's Michaela or as our sweet Boss calls her, Shmich.'

'Don't.' Short and abruptly called out. Michaela shrugged aside the extent of her annoyance as she uncrossed her legs and added a milder, 'It's a pleasure to meet you little one but

I'd prefer it if you ignored her, thanks muchly… The meanings simple enough, it just pronounces stupidly.'

'So, who cares? But an explanation would mayhap be nice.'

'Well,' Michaela reflected, giving herself time to organise how to word it by slowly bottom walking to the edge of the mat and slipping to the ground. 'It's part who I was on my original plain and part who I am aloft… Which is my hypothesis, though I can't say I've ever really bothered to ask. For to best of my recollection Bro's never called me that in front of anybody except Will prior to tonight.'

'Oh.' Underwhelmed with the brevity of Michaela's explanation, Jannelle stared at the tiny woman for a long moment then muttered a doubtful, 'That's all of it?'

'Yeah, cross my heart etcetera, etcetera. Sorry no embarrassing story there and our cute little emu chick is named Billy B.'

Three days later Jannelle threw her pen across her desk and thrust her chair back with all her strength. Having forgotten she was sitting in a float chair and not the office one she would normally use; the exotic woman swore out loud when her head banged against the panelled wall directly opposite their temporary workstations.

'Thanks sis, methinks I've had another question solved,' Michaela said as she peered over the top of her computer screen. 'Hurt much?'

'Felt, it was a pain free one, thanks anyway.' The finger Jannelle lifted to her hair moved back and forth over a rapidly stretching patch of skin as she muttered a surprised, 'Jeez I've got a lump rising already… And what's with the sis business?'

'I couldn't find you earlier this morning and I'm sure I heard an aeroplane that unless I'm mistaken, which I'm damn sure I'm not, was Palb's decrepit excuse for a plane.'

'Okay, and even if you did, it had to be his? That's one hell of a stretchy piece of gum you're chewing on girlfriend.'

'Really? You quite emphatically insisted building a landing strip was one of your department's first priorities... Something everyone, especially your mate Buster, thought decidedly strange considering we don't have any type of mechanical aircraft at the present. Annd if we've had visitors, they're our first thus very important ones, and where did they come from? Plus, if you can merge will the rest of us Mentors be able to, too? Annnd since I'm Talaa's Ambassadress why the flaming hell didn't you at least give me a buzz with your comms bracelet?'

'There's no need to shout, I'm not deaf. And enough with the flaming questions. The airfield was being pro-active and I can't be expected to remember nor know the answers to the rest of your guff.'

With a glower of disbelief, Michaela began to heat Jannelle's chair. The warmth of the seat increasing by several degrees after every tunelessly warbled word the tiny woman began to sing.

'Liar... Liar... Pants on fi...'

'You burn my butt and you'll bloody well regret it,' Jannelle growled.

'Threats? Now that's more Chiefie than JL... Are you aware old chook, your appearance keeps changing. Voice too, which makes you sound just like my sister, and mayhap I perhaps thought you looked cold.'

Although her chair had already returned to its normal

vague temperature, the set of instructions Palb had passed on were so uncompromising there was nothing she could say which would help alleviate the baffled emotions radiating off the smaller woman. Instead, the Chief Justice materialised a mirror.

Keeping her eyes firmly fixed on the reflection of her newly blonde fringe, Jannelle drifted back towards her desk whilst stating, 'Variety is said to be the spice of life.'

'Not necessarily and for pete's sake why wouldn't I want JL or the rest of the family here doofus,' Michaela snorted, before shattering Jannelle's bland silence with a less than impressed, 'Actually I'm the doofus, not thou. I've just realised Will and I are either related to or... Or are very old friends with every*one* who's turned up here. Funny I'd never really connected the dots before.'

Good enough, oh Intriguing one?

Bonzer, my pretty one.

Amused by Bro's Aussie affirmative, yet inquisitively still pondering the whys of her companion's need to verbalise her relationships, and receiving nought but a soft chuckle when she attempted to broach the topic with their Master again, Jannelle reached into the back pocket of her cargo pants, then handed the piece of recycled paper she withdrew to Michaela with a lope sided smile and a relatively serious, 'Took you long enough.'

Quickly scanning Bro's elegant copperplate Michaela echoed her earlier, 'Oh for pete's sake,' before whispering, 'I'm sorry Jannie. Perhaps you could explain all while we take a stroll around the main complex?'

The light breeze and tinge of salt that came with it tantalised

215

Michaela's senses as they walked along the pathway leading to the nearly completed building site.

'Can you smell it this time… The sea I mean?'

'Damn it, Michaela. I smelt it yesterday, the day before and the day before for that. You also know we can't go exploring until the Obs teams are back. So, for once will you please just drop it?'

'My humblest apologies, Ms Grumpy. Mayhap you'll kindly explain what happened this morning.'

'The Boss told me to go meet a plane thus I did. I shook hands with Palb, hugged and merged with JL. Palb was ropeable and left under much duress. The End… And, to add a stupid sidebar,' the Chief Justice said as she stopped to kick a wayward stone out of her way with undue force. 'We can't bloody well demerge either.'

'Sorry again.' Sincere though her apology was when Jannelle snarled at her snigger of laughter, Michaela had to swallow a few times before adding a more sympathetic, 'And no, I shouldn't think Palb would be too joyous with that, but I sure am… Um, so will I always be talking to the pair of you now or only when something changes, like for instance your hair? I not always that observant thus it might get a tad confusing…'

'Dunno but both for now and as the others keep saying, try being in our head.'

'Mmm, mayhap no thanks and are you feeling okay, 'cause you actually don't look to good.'

'Better than I was… But now it seems to come and go with the changes which is something I'll be nattering to Missy Fate about,' an unhappy Jannelle replied before JL's voice added a softly moaned, 'Which will hopefully occur sometime today. It's like being pregnant and having bloody morning sickness.'

'Ouch nasty, but how do you plan on achieving that? We haven't found a way to talk to the other plains yet... Oh.'

'Yeah oh, lord you're slow today. For if Palb can get here, something has to be open and wouldn't the Boss be honour bound to pass on a request for an a.s.a.p. meeting for us?'

'Er maybe... Maybe not, however until or even if, that can be organised. A little trip in the fresh air will probably do us all some good. Any further information we may figure out would be a bonus, three heads are better than two etc.'

'Yayas that's true and I'd prefer to keep my appearance between the three of us for now...'

'More secrets? I don't understand why that's necessary, but I guess that's between you guy's so long as you're both okay with it. Perhaps your changes will be the start of our own glitch file,' and failing to control the next lot of giggles tickling their way up her throat Michaela blurted, 'Walk?'

'It's not funny kiddo...'

'...Yet methinks our esteemed Master's suggesting we shelve all that for now,' Jannelle hurriedly threw in as she sighed then stopped and pointed. 'To take all you newbies for your first flight. Look at the bottom of the first arch.'

Swinging her eyes towards the line of Jannelle's flapping hand Michaela let out a serious of happy whoops as she jogged towards the small train parked outside the main complex's eastern entry way.

It's a grand piece of architecture, isn't it? Jannelle said, running their dual eyes over as much of the multi-purpose facility as she could see from where they now stood.

Circular in shape and rendered a pale, pinkish lilac, the

217

outer walls soared thirty metres above their heads. Its large, inset windows ensuring ample sunlight would flow into the outer levels of external work rooms and the roof-top apartments which decorated the highest one. At the base of the ground floor wall ran a four-meter wide, partially enclosed, covered glass walkway edged by beds of fine rich soil patiently waiting to be planted out.

Turning away from the train as Jannelle, with a trio of the tots scampering around her boot shod feet, entered the stone archway leading to the inner circle of buildings then the central courtyard beyond, Michaela called out, 'Aren't you lot going to come?'

'Yes... Perhaps... Maybe...'

'Whaaaaa...' Michaela spluttered, swivelling her head to peer up at a grinning Bro. 'You'll scare all the grey back into my hair if you don't stop creeping up on me.'

'Ooops,' Bro laughed, reaching behind her back to give her plait a light tug. 'Nary a grey hair in sight and if you ask nicely, I'll disappear the rest of the merge work so you can have the afternoon off.'

Gently shaking Esmeralda Magic loose from the hem of her trousers before striding over to the pair, Jannelle came to a halt in front of Bro with widespread legs and hands fisted on shapely hips. Also tipping back her head, she glared into his thickly lashed grey eyes.

'I want a meeting with Missy today,' she all but shouted. 'And what do you mean you'll lose the work? Not supposed to think tasks done when more than two of the merges are off plain... Your recommendation, remember?'

'Well, I don't recall you doing anything except the washing up last night, and Missy's undercover, thus your wee concern or whatever shall have to wait. It probably isn't that urgent,' Bro blandly refuted, although he took a hasty step backwards when Jannelle jabbed a finger into the middle of his broad chest.

'It flaming well is to us, you… You overgrown child,' she barked. 'Basic chores such as cleaning and essential cooking are covered, and exempted, by the charter… Besides Mick promised. If she wanted to do it the hard way that's her problem.'

Standing as straight and tall as she could manage whilst staring from one scowling face to the other Michaela broke in with an unusually conciliatory, 'Boss, I reckon you know it's been a pretty weird sort of morning for the Jan's and the merge work comes under a different purview. So how come we don't have to do it? And pleeease no fudging beloved.'

'Okaaaay… Okaaaay spoilt sport, I shall merely impart my news,' Bro sang as his long arms curled around the two women's waists. 'They'll be back in half an hour kiddywinks.'

The End Part One